Everything happ seemed to move trying to register could only faintly hear the screams from my friends. I was too stunned to react to what I was watching unfold before my very eyes. My brain was trying to tell me that it did not happen. Were the things I was seeing really happening? No way. Not at all. How could it have happened? This had happened before and he was perfectly fine after that. It'll all be okay. He's my best friend, after all, and we're the heroes. The heroes always win, right? You don't just lose your best friend by mere inches or milliseconds. Everything has to be alright in the end, right? Of course it does, because I'd seen him survive many times before. This wouldn't be any different.

Apparently not. Because I was watching my best friend fall to the ground with multiple holes through his body. It all happened so quickly that the blood hadn't even begun to escape him. Not until he hit the ground. The opening in his chest cavity where his heart had just been was releasing the most fluids. And, of course, his eyes were directed towards me. Of course his last image alive is that of his oldest friend in the world just standing in the distance with a blank look on his face. His right arm was reaching out to me when he landed. What could he have been reaching for? To touch me one last time? Begging for comfort? Begging for vengeance? Or begging for help in keeping him on this side of the abyss? I don't think any of those reasons mattered, because his eyes glassed over almost immediately after his body touched the earth.

Glinda had already begun casting healing spells. Her lights were firing in all directions around him like a meteor shower. She was in shock, as well, and wasn't even exactly sure what she was doing except for anything and everything within her power to save him. Unfortunately, her magic was still too weak. Should could mend the wounded but couldn't keep the dead from dying. Eric and Dorothy reacted immediately, pursuing retribution. They went after the murderer with everything they had left, which proved enough to make up for our loss. I, however, was still standing in place. All I could do was stare into my brother's frosty eyes and keep telling myself this isn't real.

None of it can be real. We're the heroes. We're the winners in our own story. We're still back home growing up. We're still hiding our misdeeds from our parents. We're still wrestling with the dogs. We're still racing home at sunset. We're still teaching each other to fight. We aren't here. We aren't fighting for our lives, countless kilometers from home. My best friend isn't dead and I'm not doing absolutely nothing about it.

Chapter 1

For my entire life, all I have known is my hometown and the immediate surrounding lands. A quaint, remote village bordering the ocean with a pleasant view of mountain ranges to the west and northwest. A river ran nearby and allowed for the farmers in the region to make a decent living. If farming or fishing didn't spark someone's interest, though, there was always the forest to the north and another farther south that held a special home for woodworkers and hunters.

With a variety of landscapes and pleasant weather, growing up in Valencia really wasn't as bad as I wanted to make it out to be. It was a small village so everyone knew each other and grew up together which meant that any kind of rumor spread like wildfire and quarrels could sometimes involve the whole town. At times, I would find any excuse possible to hate my hometown, but for anyone looking to raise a family and live in harmony, no place could be better. My friends and I, however, had no desire anytime soon to raise a family and die before it's our time.

Besides the isolation from the rest of the world, there was really only one drawback to Valencia: the monsters. According to our classes, monsters were quite abundant in the world, or, at least, in our country. Not many people have ventured beyond the kingdom's borders which isn't necessarily unusual since we only share borders with two other countries and one of them is separated by high mountains. The other country, the one two our west, is considerably smaller and does most everything on the ocean, I think. We never really learn much about the outside world in school but I do remember hearing something about the western nation exploring places beyond the Great Sea and cutting trade with us almost entirely due to some sort of disagreement or something in the past.

Valencia, my home and one of the farthest villages on the western edge of the kingdom, is in a beautiful location with much to see in every direction. The drawback in relation to the monsters, though, is that a variety of landscapes equals a variety of monsters. The guards have adapted well over the years for spotting and killing each new creature to find us, but every so often an injury or death does occur. The mountain ranges are far enough away that very few of the large flying beasts and the more durable land beasts tend not wander our way but the forests, fields, river, and ocean bring more than enough troubles on their own.

All in all, the monsters weren't actually the worst part. Being so isolated from whatever else is out there doesn't work well for kids that dream. My best friend, Adam, and I grew up dreaming together, imagining what could be out there past the fields and trees and mountains. We would lay under the stars at night and talk for what seemed like hours about what could be beyond our prison walls. And what's even more exciting is that we weren't the only ones with "delusions of grandeur" as one guard put it. Other kids in our town had similar dreams and goals to see what else could be out there. The ocean always looked especially inviting, but the adults wouldn't let children near the water. Sea creatures were typically more dangerous than those we would encounter on land. None of the warnings ever stopped us from exploring the beach from time to time and discussing ways we could sneak a boat out onto the waves. What glorious plans we once had to become the youngest boat captains in history!

Adam and I had our first run-in with a monster before we were teenagers. Another day of planning on how to make or dreams become a reality brought us to a pile of boulders on the beach, a place not unfamiliar to us but also a place we weren't allowed to be exploring alone. As we tossed rocks into the water, a clicking noise from behind startled us. I remember turning to see a large, bluish-gray crab with claws as big as my head. Luckily, Adam and I had been carrying around cheap swords for a while now and had practiced with them a number of times (which also led to a number of bruises). Adam had a rock in his hand at the time and threw it hoping to disorientate the creature, I think. Unfortunately, he missed, and by the time we could draw our swords, the crab was within claw range. The fight seemed to last an hour but it couldn't have been more than a minute. We each nearly lost a couple of limbs but through teamwork we were able to confuse the monster enough to get in the number of stabs necessary to kill it. As it died, I actually felt kind of bad. We ended up putting it out of its misery and it took a long time for me to dispel the regret of taking a life.

As time went on, we found more and more pleasure in practicing our swordsmanship with each other and ridding the borders of our village of stray beasts. By our early teenage years, however, we had to put our skills on hold and return home. My bastard father had gone away on another one of his traveling merchant deals a few years before and decided never to return which left our family, and especially mother, in shambles. When I was strong enough, all of the labor work fell to me and even some of the work raising my two siblings, Gina and Carrie. Adam tried to do some exploring on his own but found it boring so he ended up visiting quite often and helping out. That is, until his mother fell ill. We saw each other less and less the next few years.

The days of reckoning came upon our village when Adam and I reached our mid-teens. Adam's mother made a full recovery and my mom got over the worst of her grieving. My younger sister's grew up helping around the house and found that they could handle much of the day-to-day work with momma. When my best friend and I were finally set off our chains, we were starving for action. Our true, free day away from home took us into the forest where we confronted at least half a dozen flesh-hungry, giant spiders. The largest of them all must have weighed more than a grown man in armor but she died just as quickly as her minions. That was such a great day for us. We were back and more than ready to take on the world.

Often our egos would lead to reckless or risky behavior in combat. I couldn't count the number of wounds I alone received over the months after our return. It was very fortunate that we met Glinda when we did. She was so cute and sweet that you would never think she had the stomach for fighting. In all reality, she didn't, which is precisely her reasoning behind joining us: to keep us safe. Her skill set involved healing and protection magic. Having a father and mother who worked for the church in town led her to become an avid reader of the ancient holy texts in the library.

As much of a blessing as she was to have around, however, it kind of opened the door to more and more wild behavior, especially from Adam. She became such a good asset that we were convinced that we would always be okay, no matter what happened. She would have to work harder and harder to clean up our messes or keep us from creating one. But through all of the trials and tribulations she never wavered from her adorable personality. No matter what stupid thing we did, she continued to stay caring and strong.

I would have felt really bad for causing Glinda so much stress if Alice hadn't met up with us a short time later. Alice also had healing powers, but she was more adept to druidic and nature magic. Her healing spells paled in comparison to Glinda's, but she knew enough to help out in a tight spot. And if her healing spells didn't seem necessary, she could fight at least as hard as us guys.

Eric and Dorothy teamed up with us a little later. They had been really good friends for a while and doing their own thing. They came to us with two completely different personalities, which is why they worked so well together, I think. Eric is the tall, strong, silent type. Dorothy is colder and kind of mean most of the time which matches her black magic skill set perfectly. Eric is more like Glinda in the sense that he likes to protect people. He wields a spear and is bent on defending pretty much anyone or anything. While Adam and I prefer up close and personal combat, Eric prefers to fight from a distance and protect others.

Six different personalities and fighting styles. Six kids with big dreams. We really did think we were a force to be reckoned with. Those two years that we all spent together, growing together, fighting together, dreaming together was the best time of my life. Sometimes we wouldn't even hunt creatures, we would just lay in a field or play games in the forest or wade in the shallows along the beach. We would sit for hours and talk about what might be beyond the mountains and the ocean. We would sneak into the forbidden parts of the water that weren't monitored by guards to swim and play after killing off the beasts that lurked about. At least once a week we made a plan to sneak out after dark together and lay on one of the hills in the meadows and look at the stars. That was Glinda's favorite thing to do. She absolutely loved spotting shooting stars. We would make a game out of it to see who could catch the most and she always won. Stargazing suites her. Her bright personality, sparkling eyes, and gleaming smile makes me wonder if she was a shooting star that happened to fall in our village.

Exploration and combat became regular hobbies of ours quickly. Since there were six of us, we had a whole team that we truly believed could defeat anything. We would try and find a new place every time we went out, and kill any monsters we happened to find and we eventually got really good at the exterminating, too. Each of us chose a different specialty based on our personality and interests. With each new addition to our crew, it took a little more time to develop the style and teamwork that best suited us. After a couple years, though, we had become an unstoppable fighting force (or so we thought). Adam and I were the dynamic duo. Since we had been fighting together far longer, working together was like something of a choreographed dance. For a long time, our team was unstoppable.

Much of our dangerous antics had to be done in secret. We would lie and say that we were visiting the other villages or playing in the secured areas of the village limits. Anything we could think of to convince our parents that we could leave. Staying out all day, exploring and fighting occupied much of our time. For two years we had the time of our lives, growing up together and eradicating the evil that plagued the world. But, of course, our parents eventually found out what we were up to. They were obviously less than thrilled when they found out what we we had been doing. At one point, there was even a town council meeting that determined we were to remain watched within the town borders. That didn't last very long, though. We were getting very bored very fast when a pack of dire wolves caught the scent of the chickens near the edge of town and moved in. The guards are pretty tough, don't get me wrong, but they were a little more out of practice than us teenagers were. We responded quickly and eliminated five of the wolves before the rest ran off. After saving the town, the adults were more lenient to our hobbies, but there were still stipulations: not to wander too far away or to "more dangerous" areas (even though we

had already cleared many of the places named),
certain time restrictions, etc. We agreed to everything,
but we definitely didn't follow their guidelines
entirely.

Mom always worried so much about me whenever
she found out what I was doing when I left home.
Dad wasn't and hadn't been around to comfort her or
be a rock for her to lean on; that had been my job
since he decided to never come home again. It sounds
bad, but he was rarely home whenever I was growing
up anyway. He was some kind of traveling merchant
that was always going from village to village trading
and selling goods for other people. I guess he made
pretty good money because we always managed to
get by with mom doing little to no work besides
raising us kids. He would be gone for weeks at a time
and only be home for a short while. Growing up, I
really enjoyed having him home since him and I were
a lot alike and whenever mom wasn't around he
would be a lot more lenient with me. His schedule
was always sporadic so there was never any sort of
cycle we could adjust to; never knowing when he
would show up, how long he would be with us, or
how long he would be gone. Then, one day I'll never
forget, some finely-dressed men showed up at the
house and talked to mom for a while. Mom had me
take my little siblings outside during their
conversation. After they left, I went inside to ask

mom what was so important. She was at the table crying harder than I'd ever seen her cry. All she would tell me was that dad wasn't going to return ever again and that I have to be the man of the house now. She gave me very few details and always avoided the subject of him and his disappearance from our lives. Not exactly exciting news for a seven-year-old boy with two younger sisters. Over the years since then I have only managed to pull a handful of information about dad, none of which has been very useful for painting the image of who he really was but, in all honesty, I don't really care who he was. I can't respect him for what he did to mom and the rest of us. How can someone just run out on such a loving and peaceful family? I have never seen anyone love another person the way mom loved him. She always stuck by him even with his hectic work schedule. I convinced myself that I was glad that he was gone. Maybe it was true, maybe it wasn't, I don't know and I never really gave it much thought. All I knew was that mom deserved better than someone who would treat her the way he had. In the years that followed his abandonment, I tried to gradually mold myself into the proper gentleman that would raise the standard for men wishing to court my mother. I didn't want her to repeat her poor decision of putting all her heart into a man like dad.

Chapter 2

The creature crashed through the brush, knocking a small tree down as it avoided a ball of fire. It made a sharp left turn when a mass of thorny bramble roots shot up from the ground towards it. As it made it's hard turn, a spear swung at it's head. The creature barely managed to duck in time and ran off a small cliff and fell into a stream that ran through a clearing. Adam and I were already there, waiting to cut it off. The monster was a Wererat, a cross between a wolf and a giant rat. It slowly crawled to it's feet, it's red eyes glaring at us. The ugly thing started snarling and that is when I noticed something peculiar.

What looked like fumes of black smoke were coming from it's mouth. Gradually, more of the dark vapors floated from it's body. I shot a look at Adam who didn't seem to notice; he was smiling and moving towards the creature with both swords ready to strike. "Wait a minute!" I shouted as he and the creature darted toward each other. The beast fought back viciously, using sharp claws on all four limbs and an overwhelming level of agility. I rushed in to give Adam a hand, but I was hesitant to get too close before I could get a good read on the creature. This one seemed stronger and more ferocious than any other Wererat we had encountered in the past. A quick backhand from the beast took Adam off his feet. I raced to get in between them but the monster spewed some kind of black smoke from it's mouth into my face before a heavy hit to my midsection sent

13

me to the ground. I was temporarily blinded and the wind was knocked out of me but I found myself worrying about Adam and whether or not he was still vulnerable.

My vision was returning when I noticed half a dozen small, fiery explosions crash down on the creature. Eric was there immediately afterwards to jab the tip of his spear into the creature's chest. The monster only seemed more angered from the sudden intrusion and went to crush Eric's head in between both of it's paws until thorny, bramble vines shot up from the ground and wrapped around both it's wrists. Adam was up with both swords at this point and chopped off one arm at the elbow. The creature seemed unaffected and attempted to bite down on Adam's head until a bubble of light appeared around him and repelled the beast. Then I felt a warm ray of light bathe over me and suddenly I could see clearer than ever. Glinda had arrived and, as usual, had her eyes on every player in the field at once while six pixies of light hovered around her ready to execute her demands.

The monster was unusually hard to kill. Even with a severed limb it continued to operate at maximum output, which was not something these creatures typically did. It was not weird to encounter a monster that will enrage when wounded or retaliate when it's adrenaline rush kicks in. Generally, we expect that sort of behavior just in case the enemy chooses fight over flight. But Wererat's almost always hunted alone so whenever they get even moderately injured they usually take off. This one attempted to earlier but whenever we cornered it and Adam left an injury it seemed to change pace and become much more risky and violent. "I've got a bad feeling about this thing," Adam said as he ducked under a kick. Eric appeared behind the beast and smacked it with the end of his spear to knock it off balance so Alice and Dorothy could both fire blasts that sent the creature flying. All three of us guys rushed the monster as it landed only to have more of that black smokescreen hit us. Glinda immediately cast a barrier between us and the creature before firing pixies to clear the smoke. This move proved to be a smart one since the beast planned on killing all three of us at once in the midst of the distraction. Alice had magical vines shoot from different trees and tangle the three remaining limbs and neck of the monster. This gave Dorothy a chance to launch a series of magic missiles that pierced the beast's body. "How is that thing not dead yet?" Adam said looking at the struggling monster that was ignoring the new holes in it's chest cavity. "I guess that means we need to get brutal, too," he said looking at Eric and I. I didn't like the idea, but it seemed to be the only way at this point. The three of us then went to work. Glinda was opposed to the butchery and had to cover her eyes. Dorothy made sure to burn the pieces and Alice covered the ashes with dirt before we left.

"Darn, I was really hoping today wouldn't be a boring day," Alice said as we all made our way out of the woods towards home. After that bout, we were all pretty much ready to go home and relax. It was mid-afternoon and we had been out all day. "That wasn't a bad challenge," Adam said, "but it was particularly unusual. Any idea what was up with that darkness?" He was looking at Dorothy who was the only person in our group who had dabbled in dark magic. "His smokescreen attack was a lot like your Shadowball spell, Dorothy," Alice said walking up beside her.

"I noticed that but it didn't feel like any kind of the dark magic I've played around with. It was similar but there was something weird about it... Like, it almost felt alive."

"What do you mean?" I asked her.

"Well, any of the magic I've experimented with has always been hollow, so to speak. What I mean is that it doesn't ever feel like it could move on it's own if I left it sitting out, you know? It goes where I want and does what I want in a straightforward manner. The darkness that we saw earlier felt like it was operating on it's own and maybe even controlling that beast. It felt a lot like your life magic, Alice"

"My magic? But my magic has nothing to do the darkness."

"Right, but you know how your magical tendrils move about? Even though you control them and other plants it seems like they're playing around on their own, doing your bidding. That is about how that darkness felt."

"So you're saying that somebody may be controlling the darkness and possessing creatures with it from a distance?" I asked.

"I believe so," Dorothy said, "or, at least it feels like that could be a possibility."

"Well, whoever it is, all we need to do is find them and take 'em down!" Adam said. I enjoyed his enthusiasm and wanted to chime in myself but I just had this feeling that it wouldn't be that easy. It was just a curious thing that left some questions needing to be answered.

We took a couple of days off from exploring and fighting. Maybe we were all still a little shaken up, or just slightly worn out. It was kind of nice to slow down a little bit and help out around the house. My family was pretty happy to have so much of my attention. I had this weird feeling that I'd really missed them. I guess lately I'd been spending more time away than at home. The others sort of felt the same way; we were all a little reluctant to go out again, but after almost three full days at home, we were ready to stretch our muscles again.

The sun was just coming up when we met outside of town. "I kind of want to see if we run into that darkness somewhere else. You know, to see if it's, like, spreading or not," I told the group.

"That's not a bad idea," Adam say putting a hand on my shoulder, "I've been itching to go after it again."

"Is this retribution since it almost killed you last time?" Alice said, giggling.

"Shut up! I had everything under control!"

As we departed, Alice continued to take playful jabs at Adam while the rest of us laughed along.

Today, we decided to head on towards the mountain range more to the west of the jungle. We hadn't been over there much since it is pretty far away and the hills leading up to it can be a little tiring. After spending so much time at home, it felt good to do some distance walking. We didn't stop too much or for too long since this trek was longer than usual and, since it is mostly grassland between the village and the mountains, there weren't many places to sit and rest.

The creatures in the mountainous areas were a little different than our typical foes and we knew we were not entirely prepared since we hadn't traveled there much. There were larger, stronger flying monsters and the land monsters tended to be more rugged and durable. Physical strength and stamina were the two traits we had to worry about most, unlike in the forest where there is a more diverse range of abilities, such as magic, poison, and speed. We kind of enjoyed the challenge, though, and it'd been awhile since we were last there so we hoped to find ourselves more prepared than we thought.

This was by far our nastiest battle to date. Unlike with the Wererat, the darkness had completely taken over the eagle causing its size and strength to double. It was so fast and hit so hard that us guys couldn't land a hit and every time it would swoop in close and we'd try to get ahold of it, it would just knock us off our feet. Eric was the first to sustain a serious injury; the eagle's talons ripped his back wide open. Glinda and her pixies were on the scene immediately. She sent him an aura of light that gradually healed his wounds over a period of time and then a handful of pixies appeared to repair the bulk of the damage. He had to find cover momentarily so Dorothy made a distraction by sending out a bunch of tiny fireballs, like flares, directly at the eagle's head. The distraction proved effective but the eagle flew directly up until its senses refocused.

Alice tried to take advantage of its disorientation by using her magic to fling a bunch of stones at the beast, but a couple large flaps of its wings sent the stones right back and she had to use wind magic to deflect them. Her defensive spell was not strong enough, however, and she received some minor cuts on her arms and legs. She tended to her own wounds while Glinda finished up with Eric. Dorothy made an effort to hit the beast with a fireball spell while it was focused on Alice but to no avail. This whole time, Adam and I were looking around for ways we can get to it but the creature was smart enough not to hover too close to anything at all.

"If it wasn't so far away and good at defending itself from ranged attacks I could throw a spinning sword at it," Adam said, grinding his teeth out of frustration.

"Alice!" I shouted, "is there any way you can ground it with your vines and brambles?"

"I can't use the spell this far away from vegetation!" she informed us. That was news to me; we had always been pretty close to trees whenever I'd seen her use it, now that I thought about it.

The monster swooped down, this time much faster, with darkness radiating from its body. It was heading right for Glinda, who began preparing a shield spell. Her spell was not forming quickly enough and the creature's dive bomb was nearing its target. Luckily, Eric had finished healing and scooped the enchantress up in both arms, leaving his spear behind. His reaction was well-timed, as the two had barely enough time to avoid the earth-shattering impact that sent rubble, the spear, and our friends flying in different directions. The eagle stood itself up, completely unphased by the heavy crash. Adam was already on the scene, throwing his sword and using a bit of magic to cause it to spin at a high speed. Luckily, the beast had just stood up and hadn't gotten a good look around yet so the attack managed to take it by surprise, striking a part of its wing. By this time, Adam was preparing to hit it with his other sword when the eagle's other wing struck him in the head, sending him flying into the mountainside. Dorothy and Alice took the chance and fired off a series of spells but the creature managed to block most of them with its wing. A few spells managed to hit but hardly affected the beast at all. It began taking flight when Eric jumped and grabbed ahold of its right leg. The eagle was enraged and flapped its wings harder to get airborne. I was making sure Adam was okay when I noticed what Eric was doing. "Eric!" I shouted as I threw my sword at him. He stretched out his arm but just barely missed catching it as the eagle took him higher and higher.

Glinda was firing a number of little pixies to circle around Eric so they could heal him temporarily in case he sustained any damage. "Alice, can you use a twister spell to send one of us up there after them?" I asked as I helped Adam to his feet. "My magic isn't strong enough to get anything up to them now," she said fretfully.

Eric was trying to climb up the beast's back as it used its other leg to scratch at him. One of his arms and a leg was cut open as he made his way past its thigh. The eagle swooped up and down in different directions and spun upside down to try and knock the annoyance off. Eric wrapped his arms around its neck to try and choke it, but nothing seemed to affect it. He finally remembered that he carries a dagger. He rarely ever uses it, since he has generally focused on defense over offense. He reached for it but when the creature felt his grip loosen, it began spinning in a spiral. Eric desperately grabbed a handful of feathers but after the third of fourth roll, the feathers came out and he was left with one arm barely around the beast's neck. Eventually, the eagle managed to knock him off but Eric's still outstretched left arm allowed his hand to connect with the base of the left wing and he was able to hold on.

On the ground, we were preparing a spell for the next close encounter. Alice was charging a vortex of wind energy while Dorothy was creating a razor-sharp shard of ice. The two were going to combine their spells to fire the ice directly into the creature's body. "Make sure you have it as sharp as you possibly can, Dorothy, the dark energy surrounding the monster is protecting it from the bulk of explosive-related spells," I coached. Adam had both swords ready to throw to distract the monster and Glinda had light magic ready in each hand. "Adam, when I give the signal, throw both spinning swords in an arc, coming from each side, with one going to the head and the other to the body."

When the eagle stopped rolling, Eric adjusted himself on its back and pulled out his dagger. He stabbed the abomination as hard as he could at the base of its neck. The eagle let out an ungodly screech and, out of fury or desperation, caused the darkness radiating off of its body to explode out. The shock was enough to knock Eric unconscious, as well as the monster. Both fell from the sky, accelerated by the force of the blast. "Alice, slow his fall!" I shouted, running to where Eric would land. Dorothy stopped charging her spell and ran towards the falling monster, ready to shoot what she had prepared. Alice and Glinda followed me while Adam accompanied Dorothy.

Luckily, Eric wasn't falling too far away, and Alice was able to almost completely slow his fall with her wind magic. Glinda began healing him before he even made it to the ground where I caught him and laid him down to rest. I left him in Glinda's care while Alice and I went to join the other two.

The eagle recovered quicker than Eric did, and managed to stop its own fall, but not before two spinning blades came down upon it. The monster barely avoided both, but was surprised by a sparkling blue dart that struck it directly in the chest. The eagle screeched and flailed as it crashed down on the other side of a group of boulders. Alice and I joined up as the beast landed so we split into the teams and made our way around each side of the boulders.

What we saw on the other side stopped us immediately. It seemed as if the darkness was trying to heal the creature, causing threads of skin to dance around the hole made by Dorothy. What looked like muscle strands were filling into the hole from other areas of the monster's body. The creepiest thing was that there was no blood to be found anywhere. "This is a disgusting display of magic," Dorothy said, "we'd better do something fast." Adam was on the same page and made his way towards the monstrosity. Alice had to cover her mouth and nose. "It smells awful," she said.

I went down the hill to join Adam where him and I approached the beast slowly in case the darkness chose to act on its own, as we'd seen before. "Let's decapitate it," Adam told me. "You go for it with both swords, I'll go after the gaping hole to distract the darkness," I replied. When Adam was ready, I jumped forward and stabbed the wound. Tendrils of darkness and muscle fibers shot out at me, leaving a series of piercings across my body and flinging me backwards. My distraction proved useful, however, because when I looked up, Adam was throwing the monster's head away while the beak tried to chomp an arm off. Dorothy immediately set the head ablaze. The last thing I saw was the darkness evaporate above the body and float there for a moment before exploding towards each of us.

I woke up to an emerald green light bathing over me. As I opened my eyes I heard Alice say, "he's awake!" I looked around to find Glinda healing Dorothy and Adam while Eric inspected the remains of the eagle.

It was not yet twilight, but the sun was starting to go down as we made our way down the cliffside.

"There's no way we'll make it back before dusk," Adam said.

"Sorry we kept you out past your bedtime," Alice replied, "but I promised your mommy I would take good care of you." Adam joined in on the playful insults that ended in Alice kicking him in the butt and running off.

"Don't forget to invite us to the wedding," Glinda called out to them. I rather enjoyed how we could have fun like this even after an epic battle that nearly left us dead.

"What are you grinning about?" Dorothy asked me. We were at the back of the group as we made our way off the base of the mountain.

"Oh, nothing, I just hope we're like this forever," I told her.

"That's an awfully bold thing to say," she told me. "We won't be young kids forever, you know?"

"I know that, but, I mean, friends like this. Like, this kind of friendship and playfulness is rare, and I don't want to lose that."

"I understand," she said, "but in our profession, that can be a lot to ask for. We can't continue to fight to the brink of death and still hold onto our joy forever."

"I guess you're, right. Maybe we should consider hanging up our swords permanently as soon as we solve the mystery of this darkness."

Eric overheard our conversation and turned to say, "as long as there is evil in the world, darkness or not, we'll have to take action. We won't be able to get any rest."

"What makes you say that?" I asked the usually silent giant.

"We have a power that most people do not have, so when an evil rises up and other's cannot protect themselves, we will have to fight." I pondered that ideal for a while as we all walked back. Dorothy and Eric brought up the rear, engaging in their usual small talk, while I continued forward, lost in my thoughts about our future as a group. *Is that really our destiny?* I wondered to myself. *Will this fighting never end?*

"Are you lost, young man?" A soft voice broke the spell I was under. I looked over to see Glinda's sparkling blue eyes staring up at me. I didn't have anything to say right away so she broke the silence, "isn't this beautiful?" I didn't know what she was referring to, but I was still looking at her; her platinum blonde hair and red lips. "Yes," I squeaked, my voice cracking slightly. Then I realized that we were at the crest of a hill and she was looking across the landscape. The sun was just below the horizon and some of the stars were out. She had been admiring the scenery and I was a little embarrassed that I had been too busy staring at her beauty than noticing what she had actually been talking about. My face got a little red but I don't think she noticed. "I don't like fighting, by any means, but I do love to explore and see new sights, and my favorite times are when we can be playful and fun like this," she said as we watched Alice and Adam push each other back and forth. She had been thinking the same things that I had been worrying about.

"I agree," I told her, "I had just been thinking about how I hope we can always be together like this."

"I like to wish that, too," she said as she looked down, "but I'm not so sure that'll be the case." She became more glum and she mentioned things that closely resembled what Dorothy and Eric had said to me earlier. Had I been the only one to avoid a darker truth and hide myself in blissful thoughts? I couldn't help but wonder if bliss could be a reality or if peace was just some sort of fantasy that I was trying to convince myself of.

It was well after dark when we met up with a handful of guards from the village. Since we had left so early and had been out longer than ever today, our parents threw a fit and the mayor called for teams of guards to go out searching for us. We were escorted directly to the town hall to confront our furious guardians and the town council. "What in the hell makes you kids think you can go off like that, endangering yourself and possibly others?" The mayor yelled and scolded us for an unusually long time, not even giving any of us a chance to speak. Then each of our parents took turns yelling at us before turning the meeting back over to the mayor. "This council has already come to a decision that you six will not be allowed to leave the borders of this town ever again without an escort."

We each jumped up, all shouting our own points of contention. The mayor's rapped his gavel furiously on the desk. "Silence!" he shouted, "there will not be a discussion on the matter!" "But, sir, we've discovered something that may be of dire concern to the village," I said, stepping forward. The room got quiet and then the mayor asked me what I meant by that. So then we all went on describing our latest couple of adventures.

Chapter 3

The sun was high in the air and it had been gradually getting hotter and hotter in this jungle as the days went on. The trees blocked out much of the sun but the air was so damp that it felt as if we were constantly walking through spiderwebs of water. "We found the road!" Adam called from up front. Him and one of the town guards were using their swords to create a path through the dense vegetation. We had been on the road the other day but had to make a detour when the rain caused some flooding and then found ourselves lost. The roadway hadn't been used as much in the past decade as before so a number of plants moved in to populate the smooth ground.

Our mayor had grown increasingly worried over the past few months when communications with the nearest city to the north pretty much ceased. Apparently, our mayor and the other had always kept a steady line of information flow with couriers at least once a month. For whatever reason, no matter what, a message was sent between town halls once a month at the very least. It had been nearly two months and even though our mayor has sent a couple couriers, the other mayor has not sent one in return. The first courier made contact but claimed to have been stopped by a guard upon arrival where he was told to hand over the message and was then sent back empty-handed. The last courier was sent a week ago and still has not returned.

That is how us and four of the town guards ended up lost in the forest. Our mission was to investigate the missing courier, gather intelligence on the unknown status of the town, hand deliver an urgent message to the mayor, and report back within one week. It was now midday on the third day of our quest and we were still a few hours out, so we only had one full day of investigation. Given that everything on our to-do list is in the same spot, however, we shouldn't need the whole day. I was just ready to sleep in a bed and eat some quality food.

Eric was the only member of our group who seemed to fit in with the town guards. Each man was taller and more muscular than the average guy; a requirement to protect the village. They also carried heavier weapons than we were accustomed to and wore chainmail armor under their leather. Adam and I looked more like children next to each of them. I hoped to one day resemble any one of them, but for now, I just felt more insecure about my own self. I decided that I just needed to work harder and keep their physique in mind as a goal to work towards.

The detour we made really hurt us but we finally arrived at the town of Castelle at sunset. The town is about twice the size as ours–they participated in a lot more trading since they aren't as isolated as our village is.

"Do you guys notice anything peculiar?" the head guard said to us as we approached the edge of the city.

"It looks… deserted," Alice replied.

"Be on your guard," Eric said. We all drew our weapons and kept our heads on a swivel as we passed through the rows of buildings.

The city was more compact than ours and made that work by having all their buildings touching and lining the roadways. Many places, such as restaurants and bakeries, had tables and chairs outside for people to eat and socialize. The buildings were all three or four floors high with apartments occupying the upper floors. Many of the apartments had small balconies and almost every window had flowers or other plants growing outside. "This is a pretty town," Glinda said, admiring the horticulture. None of us had ever been here before, and the scenery was truly worth appreciating.

The sunset cast an eerie orange glow across the rooftops and the shadows between buildings grew larger as time passed. We didn't see a single living (or unliving) creature on our way to the town center. The town hall was a large, stone building with an elaborate exterior and statues of past leaders lining the roof. It was attached to an enormous cathedral that was so beautiful we were all forced to stop and marvel at its design. "Let's make an appointment to go in there later," Adam said. "I agree," I said, "but only after we find someone to enlighten us on the situation here."

We had to break open the doors to the town hall and what we discovered inside was the most puzzling thing thus far. There was nothing. Not just no people, but there were no documents anywhere in the hall or in the offices indicating any kind of exodus, plague, or invasion. We broke into the cathedral next to find the same lack of clues. The bishop's personal study even contained no sort of record as to any recent events. "Look here," the head guard said, pointing to a page in a book on the bishop's desk. The book was a calendar and the last recording was nearly two months ago. All it said was the type of church service that had been performed that morning.

"It's as if this entire town was constructed but never inhabited," one of the guards said as we all gathered outside by a retired fountain. "It's kind of creepy," Alice said. It was nighttime now and a large crescent moon hung in the sky, faintly lighting up the surrounding buildings. Structures not bathed in the glow turned into shadowy figures. Moonlight reflected on various objects throughout the town turning them into tiny eyes that watched us intently, never blinking. "Our best bet would be to stay here for tonight and leave a more in-depth investigation for the morning," the head guard said. "We might as well find an inn and see if there is any food that hasn't gone bad." He had two of the guards go inside the town hall and search for a map of the city. Dorothy went with them to use her fire magic as a light source.

We sat on the small steps that outlined the fountain for quite some time. We didn't talk much; we were each pondering the situation, running through every possibility for the absence of life. Had monsters come and wiped out the residents? Could there be any that strong? Was the darkness involved with this? These questions and more ran through our heads.

As we sat in silence, we began to hear the occasional bump and thud. I figured it was just my imagination until a particularly conspicuous knock sounded behind us. I turned to see Adam and Eric sitting on the fountain in that direction. Adam was turning to look at me. "Was that you?" He asked me. "I was going to ask you the same thing. I thought maybe you guys were throwing rocks or something." "It wasn't us," Adam said, "I heard it from your direction. Like someone tapped on wood."

"Calm down, kids," the head guard told us. "It's just the sounds of the night and your imaginations making more than what it really is."

"But…" Eric began, "aren't the sounds of the night usually caused by animals or bugs?" The head guard thought about that for a moment and was about to respond until the doors to the town hall burst open.

"Alright, which one of you was it?" One of the guards said angrily.

"What are you talking about?" I asked him.

"Don't play dumb," Dorothy said. "We know at least one of you was in there, too. We even saw you!"

They came over to us, pretty upset about one of us apparently sneaking in there and making spooky noises. Dorothy said she shot a small fireball at the wall in the direction of one noise and they saw the shadow of a figure dart around the corner and disappear.

"It wasn't any of us," Adam said. "We were just talking about the weird noises that we'd been hearing when you guys showed up."

"Alright, enough of this silly bantering," the head guard said. "Let me see the map and let's go get some sleep."

The nearest inn was only a couple blocks away. The walk there was unnervingly creepy. The moonlight created many shadows and the reflections continued to watch us from every corner. Even with the head guard's stern attitude and bold presence, we were all still a little on the edge. His pace seemed to quicken as time went on. Every turn and every alleyway caused at least one of us to do a double-take due to the detection of possible movement. There was never anything there, though. Or so we thought. Or hoped.

We finally made it to the deserted inn and even the head guard let out a very faint sigh of relief. While a couple guards searched for food, the rest of us found ourselves rooms, bedding materials, and the baths. Before doing any of that, though, we lit every candle and every torch in the building. The guards came back from the kitchen and the cellar to report that there was no food. "None at all?!" Alice yelled before flopping down on the couch. "I'm gonna die!"

"Good," Adam said with a chuckle. Luckily for him, Alice was too tired and hungry to say anything, so she just threw her shoe with minimal effort.

"Don't worry," said one of the guards. "We still have plenty of leftovers from the trip here. We can always search for more food tomorrow." The 'leftovers' he referred to didn't excite any of us. They were nothing more than some loaves of bread, some vegetables, and salted meat. At least we could cook some of it in the kitchen.

"Alright, listen up," the head guard said to everyone after dinner. "We'll do one hour watch shifts throughout the night. There are seven men, which will get us past sunrise. Everyone sleep with their equipment nearby and be ready for anything. Keep the windows locked but all the doors open. Everyone sleeps at least two to a room. I'll be the first to watch and I'll write down where everyone is sleeping and the order of the shifts." None of us were excited about waking up for an hour at night, but I had a feeling that none of us will be getting much sleep anyway.

I jerked awake, sitting up and drawing my knife out of reflex. I looked to my right to see Eric standing by me. "Is it my turn already?" I whispered, trying not to wake up Adam on the other side of the bed. "It's five in the morning," Eric said, "the sun will be coming up soon. You have the unfortunate next-to-last shift." I rubbed my eyes and slapped my cheeks. I don't remember falling asleep but I remember tossing and turning for what seemed like hours on end. I think I had been dreaming about movement in the shadows when Eric shook me awake.

I met Eric in the lobby a few minutes later. He had some cold water for me to splash on my face. "Ugh," I moaned as I wiped my face with a rag. "I feel like I didn't get any sleep at all."

"Here, drink this in one gulp," he said as he handed me a tiny glass of clear liquid. I did as he instructed and nearly threw up. Whatever that was burned like fire in my mouth and all the way down to my stomach.

"What the hell was that?!" I tried to shout through coughs.

"It's some kind of liquor that the second-shift guard found. Wakes you right up, doesn't it?" He was smiling. I could feel my body warming up. My head swayed a little bit and I felt kind of dizzy. I had never had liquor before.

"Don't drink anymore," he told me as he left the room.

The chosen seat for watch duty was by the fireplace facing the main entrance and the front desk. The inn was a very comfortable and welcoming place. The candles had died down but some torches along the walls seemed to have been relit earlier. I was admiring the decorations as I wondered what on earth could have happened here. I hoped that our questions would be answered in the coming hours. I guess I got very lost in my thoughts because my shift was nearly over when I caught a glimpse of light cascading through the windows. I looked at the clock above the fireplace and found it to be almost time to wake Adam up. He got lucky to get the last shift; there was no way I would fall back to sleep, and if I did I would be so drowsy when I woke up again at seven.

Adam was snoring when I went to wake him up. He had an arm and leg around my pillow and was drooling on it. I sat down my sword and took a deep breath before shaking him furiously whispering loudly, "wake up! Wake up! Wake up!" He jolted up, hair a mess, and his left hand caught my nose. That wasn't enough to stifle my chuckles. "Shh," I said. "Eric is asleep!"

"You're a mythological ass," he said, rubbing his eyes. "I was having a great dream about…"

"About… Alice?"

"Your mother," he said at the same time I mentioned Alice's name and then started to laugh at his own joke until he registered what I'd said but he was still too sleepy and yawned instead of retaliating.

After he took his position in the lobby I gave him the shot of liquor and he coughed some of it back up. He tried to hit me but I laughed and ran off upstairs. When I took one look at the bed he destroyed, I grabbed another blanket and laid it over the entire bed and got myself a new pillow and made every effort to focus on just relaxing a little bit.

"Wakey wakey!" I heard as a heavy weight crashed over me. I woke up to find Alice on top of me. "I could've lived the rest of my life without that," I wheezed as she climbed off. "What time is it?" "It's after eight. We let you snooze a little longer while we all got ourselves ready. Now hurry up, breakfast is ready and I'm hungry!"

I met everyone else downstairs and they had already started eating. I took my place and had the meager meal that was prepared; we were running low on food and our first priority while we were here was to find more. "We've got plenty of hours in the day to scour this city and find some food and some clues. We'll break up into teams to cover the maximum amount of ground. Keep an eye on the clock tower and we'll meet outside the town hall at noon to pool our findings," the head guard said as we were all getting our things together. We then broke into five teams of two and were then assigned a section of the city to explore. Then the head guard gave a quick inspection of each person as they walked out the door and from there we were off on our own for a few hours of fun.

Chapter 4

Adam had been inspecting a couple of food carts down a side road, that was little more than an alleyway, when he noticed that his companion was missing and he had been talking to himself. "Alice?"

he called out a few times, looking around. The nearest doorway, a little farther down the shaded street, was to some kind of shop. The outside wall was lined with windows and no sign of recent human activity could be found beyond them. Adam poked his head inside the building and once again called out to his friend. He stepped back to scan the road once more and deduced that, if she had gone to look at anything else, this must be where she went. He took a step inside and put a hand on one sword.

The wall of windows helped to illuminate all but two open doorways. One doorway was behind the front counter and the other was in the back corner. "Alice!" he shouted this time. "Of course the one person here who can make light ends up disappearing," he grumbled as he approached the nearest doorway. Sword drawn, hand shaking, Adam went on to stab a couple times into the room. "This is silly," he laughed to himself. He then poked his head inside and looked around. It took a little bit for his eyes to adjust but what he could make out was an office where the store owner must've kept his records. Adam went to the desk, still shaking from the excitement he'd caused himself, and grabbed a handful of papers that were lying out. He took them back into the light and found that they contained no information on the sudden vacancy.

"This one must be some kind of storage room," Adam said to himself as he approached the other doorway. This time, he didn't stab his sword in. As he took a step inside, a white face with huge eyes appeared in front of him and a loud squeal came with it. Adam screamed, dropping his sword, and falling back into a shelf. Alice, laughing hysterically, took off her head a flour bag that had the painting of a bunny on it. "Y-your," she struggled to say, hunched over laughing and holding her sides. "Your face is priceless!" She was crying as the words came out sporadically. "I'm going to kill you!" Adam said, picking up his sword and drawing the other one, as Alice sat down to laugh more. He decided to spare her life this time, but he chose not to speak to her until she started to tell all of us the story when we later met up. He was struggled to keep a hand over her mouth as she spat the story out between fits of laughter.

"Do you have a bad feeling about all of this?" I could tell that Glinda had been a little on edge since we first entered the town, so when she asked me, again, if I have any strange or bad feelings, I made sure to assure her, again, that it is a weird situation but I don't have any bad feelings. I most certainly did, however, but there was no way I was telling her that.

We were searching through the fourth large house of the day. The section we were assigned contained what seemed to be an upper-class district of citizens. We had no trouble navigating the larger houses since Glinda had summoned a small army of light pixies to highlight all the corners of each room.

At first, I was pretty happy to inspect these houses since I was sure there would be a study of some sorts that contained journals or writings of recent events. In all honesty, though, these homes were larger and nicer than any I could've imagined and I really just wanted to revel in their beauty. So far, my theory had been proven wrong. It seemed as if the entire town literally stopped everything they were doing one day and left with all the food in the village. One journal I found had a final entry dating back to, once again, about two months ago and it revealed no clues whatsoever to the lack of residents.

We continued down the neighborhood with no more luck than when we began. At the last house on our stop before we needed to head back, I found myself alone in a bedroom on the top floor. "Glinda?" I called out only to receive silence. The last I knew, she was in the room next to mine, but when I went out into the hall, the only pixie I found was the one stationed outside my own room. There were no more fairies in any of the upstairs rooms or down the staircase. "Did you see where she went?" I asked the pixie outside my room. It couldn't speak, but it made a gesture indicating it had no clue as to what happened. I began to get very worried. "Glinda!" I shouted as I quickly made my way downstairs.

There were no more pixies to be found in the rest of the house besides the four that were accompanying me. Before, we'd have multitudes of pixies populating each building we entered, but now that number had been reduced to four. The house was filled with large windows that allowed a decent amount of sunlight to come in and but I still relied on my pixies to help me reinspect as much of the building as possible.

Finally, I made my way to the basement door. We had looked down there before and found it barren; a half-dozen rooms with empty shelves lining the walls and empty barrels filling the corners. There was a lot of surface area and I remember that earlier we had to use more than thirty pixies to illuminate the whole place. With my four, I couldn't even light most of the main room.

The little floating lights did little to help me. In some of the smaller rooms, they created more shadows than they denied. I kept at least one pixie in the doorways for security. Things were still creepy, but at least I could detect a change in the light. Each pixie kept an eye on each other, as well, so I could be notified if any of them noticed anything suspicious. I carefully searched each room and found nothing. I came to the final room to find the door to it was shut. It was odd, because I didn't remember shutting any doors today. I drew my sword and told three of the pixies to dart in immediately. I kicked out the door and watched the pixies go in and fire around the room then I charged in behind them. Unfortunately (or luckily), there was nothing to be found. Glinda or I must've closed the door without thinking about it. We left the basement, leaving that door open this time.

I continued calling out to Glinda as I made my way to the front door. I walked around outside for a little bit when I noticed something that we missed earlier. I made my way to the side of the house and found a fence of hedges and a wooden door. I assumed it must lead to the backyard of the house. I opened the door and walked down the narrow pathway between the exterior of the home and a hedge wall to find myself in a beautiful garden. I hadn't seen anything like this before. *This seems like the kind of place Glinda would end up*, I thought to myself. Sure enough, a pixie appeared in front of me and beckoned me to follow it.

Near the back of the garden, lying on a stone bench and surrounded by an array of gorgeous flowers that I'd never even seen in my dreams, was Glinda. She was sound asleep, her golden hair cascading over her arms that were tucked under her head to cushion her from the hard surface. She was curled up and looked so peaceful that I felt bad to wake her. "Hey," I said softly as I gently shook her shoulder. "Glinda." She slowly regained consciousness. She was very surprised when she began registering everything. "Oh! Oh my! Was I asleep?" Her shock didn't stop a yawn.

"You don't remember coming here and taking a nap?"

"Well, I remember coming here. I told you I was going down to the garden behind the house."

I must've had a puzzled expression on my face because then she said, "did you not hear me?"

"No," I said before telling her of my own adventure.

"That is so strange because I swear I said something. I came out here to look around and the last thing I remember is taking a seat here to admire the flowers. Suddenly, you're waking me up."

This was an unusually strange circumstance and became even more so when she told me that she left all the pixies around the house when she came out. " I'm so sorry," she finally said after a few moments of silence. "I didn't mean to scare you, really."

"Maybe you were more sleepy than you realized and dismissed the pixies without knowing it. That would explain why you fell asleep so quickly and don't remember." I tried to console her but I was very worried. Glinda was much too responsible and thoughtful to do something like this. Maybe something serious really was going on in this village.

"We should get back," I said with a smile as I helped her off the bench. "We don't need you causing everyone else any worry!"

"That's not funny!" She said as she pushed me.

We were the last team to meet at the fountain.

Chapter 5

I woke up to screams. At least, I think I did. I was sleeping very deeply, catching up from the last few nights, and having a weird dream. Men and women alike screaming jumbled sentences. Then I started coughing furiously. I started to gag, ready to throw up, and then my eyes shot open. Back in my bed, all I could see was a thick, gray haze. I rolled off the bed to the floor where the smoke, responsible for my hacking, hadn't accumulated yet and then I realized that the screams were real. "Let's go, idiot!" A figure shouted through the fog. Adam was crouched down in the doorway with a rag over his face. I grabbed my stuff and followed.

Everyone was meeting across the road at this pavilion that we determined earlier had been used as a outdoor restaurant for travelers. As I ran, I turned to see almost the entire inn up in flames. The head guard was conducting a body count as Adam and I showed up. We were the last to arrive and I was embarrassed that I'd slept through the chaos. Once the head guard confirmed one-hundred percent accountability, he unleashed upon another guard a fury as violent as the flames that were consuming the inn. Apparently, the second-shift guard had fallen asleep all through his shift and into the next and allowed a fire to begin on the base floor and build itself to an unstoppable level before the smoke finally woke him.

"See that?" I overheard Dorothy say to Eric. I followed their gaze up to the sky.

"I don't see anything," Eric replied.

"Exactly." Dorothy was right. Last night, a thick crescent moon had lit up the sky for us. Now, there was nothing. No moon, and no stars. Eric grabbed his spear and walked into the road. Dorothy followed him with her wand.

"What are you doing?" The head guard took a break from shouting at his subordinate to shout at them.

"Look at the sky," I said to him. He did, and after a few moments of turning the wheels in his brain he yelled at all of us to get our equipment on and be alert.

"Everyone, stay on the pavilion and do not leave the light of the fire!" We were all ordered to break up the wooden tables and chairs on the pavilion so they could be set on fire if we needed them to. The pavilion was bordered on three sides by buildings so we could hold ourselves in a defensive position with little worry, as long as nothing comes at us through the restaurant to our backs.

Eric and Dorothy were still out in the road. When they were called back, Eric was the last to retreat. He was walking backwards and his shadow from the firelight was long. As he backed up, his shadow touched another shadow that was created from an empty cart in the road. I was at the edge of the pavilion and watching him when I noticed the cart. It hadn't been there before, and neither had all the other carts, barrels, and other stuff that was now lining the road on both sides. His shadow had been touching the other one for only a couple seconds when a jet of darkness shot up from his feet and through his body, disappearing into the air above. "Eric!" I shouted as he fell to his knees. Glinda was quick to cast a healing spell. Dorothy and I ran to him. She cast a fireball in each direction down the road. We didn't see anything but as soon as Glinda's spell finished, another darkness repeated the same event. And then another. Eric collapsed to the ground before we could react. Glinda and Alice both fired a healing spell this time but Eric was unconscious and barely breathing. Adam and another guard came and helped me pick him up. "Get him back here!" the head guard yelled. "And you, too," he said to Dorothy.

"Dorothy, fireball that window!" Adam yelled, pointing at one along the wall bordering the pavilion. She did without hesitation.
"Over here!" said a guard pointing at a window on the other building. Alice was on this one.
"Halt! We're still in the light; they're keeping to the shadows so we're safe for now," the head guard was checking on Eric as he called commands.

"How long do you think that fire is going to burn?" Dorothy asked as she prepared a fireball in each hand. "This village is deserted so what do you say we set another fire and keep that process going until sunrise?"

The head guard wasn't too keen on the idea of burning down a whole town. There were reasons to keep the blaze going, but at least as many reasons not to. Homes, businesses, records… so many things, people's entire lives, were scattered across these buildings. "We can't burn down the city," he finally told us. "And we're going to have to stop that fire eventually; it's already spreading." He was right, in a few more minutes there won't be any need for Dorothy to start another fire. The entire city block will go down in flames by the end of the night.

As we watched the fire and our surroundings, we all became increasingly aware of movement in the windows around us. Taps on the glass, scratches on the walls, and knocks on wood haunted us. "Hey, there's something here," the guard watching the restaurant behind us was approaching the doorway. "Was this door always open?"
"Don't get too close!" Then his shadow touched the darkness inside the door and he was pulled inside by his feet so quickly that none of us could take action. We heard him scream in a kind of agony that no person should ever experience and then he was quiet. "It was his shadow!" I told everyone how I had

noticed Eric's shadow touch another before he got hurt, and after seeing this I was sure they were attacking us through our shadows.

"So you figured it out. Well done," a deep, slightly raspy voice said to us from the road as we were all fixated on the restaurant.   I felt a chill run down my spine and my heart raced faster. I didn't recognize this voice. When we all turned around, we were presented with a finely dressed, older gentleman who was standing in front of the collapsing inn. Darkness was radiating from him as we had seen with the Wererat and the eagle. "You're all stunned, that is to be expected. Allow me to introduce myself: I am the mayor of this town. You can just call me Mayor," he said with a bow. "You must have so many questions and I would be pleased to answer as many as I can if you would please accompany me to my hall."

"We won't be going anywhere with you!" the head guard shouted as he pulled out his bow and pointed an arrow directly at the Mayor. "You'll tell us everything we want to know standing right there."

The Mayor only grinned. "Young man, you are no longer in charge. I am merely extending a beneficial opportunity to you."

"Beneficial for whom?" Dorothy shouted as she stepped forward, ready to cast her fireball spells. The Mayor only sighed. The grin returned to his face as he began to step forward. He only took two steps before the head guard released the arrow right into the Mayor's chest. He only took one step back and then laughed before ripping out the arrow. There was no blood. The darkness filled in the hole in his body until nothing was left to show of the wound besides a hole in his shirt.

With a snap of his finger, the Mayor became circled by reinforcements. Two dozen villagers appeared from the the buildings to our left and right and huddled around their leader. They were all radiating darkness. "You see," he began. "We don't need to hide in the shadows. We have the shells we need to bar the light."

"We can't fight human beings, can we?" Alice asked.

"They're going to kill us if we don't," Adam said.

"Don't kill them!" the head guard said. "Try and immobilize them; we may be able to restore them to their real selves!"

"My apologies, but there is no hope of that even if you survive this," the Mayor said. With that, the people, armed with sticks, farm equipment, or just their fists, charged at us.

"Through the restaurant! Girls!" With the command, Dorothy, Glinda, and Alice were the first to go, firing different spells to clear a pathway of lights. Instead of wasting time to navigate through the building, Dorothy blasted the back wall with fire before Eric and a guard charged it to break through. Up until this very moment, our plan was solid for being desperate and spontaneous… but now we were blocked from the light of the burning inn. It was very obvious that yellow eyes were fixed on us as soon as we appeared in the darkness.

Glinda was the quickest and produced a plethora of pixies instantly. It was a great move but it came at a cost. She immediately dropped to a knee. One of the guards picked her up and put her on his back after his boss ordered him to. Eric and another guard who also carried a spear were covering the hole in the restaurant we had just created. They were using the ends of their spears to smack at the villagers' heads or chests in the hopes of knocking them out but the darkness seemed to have made them stronger and resistant to unconsciousness.

We took a left to head back in the direction of the town hall. We hadn't originally planned on that, but as we were running we remembered how fortified the infrastructure in that area was so we began developing a plan to barricade ourselves inside until morning. Both the hall and the cathedral were mostly stone and were even augmented with metal roofs. The primary concern would be windows or any access from underground, which we figured was possible.

Thanks to Glinda's pixies, the shadows were kept at bay. Each person had some orbiting their body, while even more were orbiting our entire group, and just for good measure, there were some floating farther out. All the lights touched each other so no shadows could get in between. Everything was going just fine and we were closing in on the city center.

We were only seconds from breaking free of the rows of buildings when possessed villagers started jumping down from the rooftops and out of windows. We shrugged off the surprise and prepared to defend ourselves while still moving forward as quickly as possible but it eventually became clear that we were not the primary targets. The reckless crowd attacked the pixies first. Handfuls of lights began to disappear at once. Glinda was still wore out and we were becoming vulnerable.

The mob was approaching dangerously fast and the dark creatures were creeping in and beginning to surround us. We couldn't knock the villagers unconscious quickly enough so the head guard made a frantic call that we should immobilize them any way possible while trying our best not to kill them. Then I saw Adam cut off someone's leg, and then one of the guards jammed his spear into another's arm. A villager came up behind me yelling and bringing a large piece of wood down towards my head so I sliced his arm off at the elbow. Dorothy lit someone on fire, Alice smashed a man's head in between two stones, and Eric threw one villager through a window. Desperate for our lives, we didn't react in the most humane of ways, but after a matter of seconds we had saved ourselves with about half of our pixies to spare. Huddling closer together we sprinted towards the finish line with the vicious mob barely one building length behind us.

The group was throwing stuff at us. None of the throws were very accurate but they were things like daggers, knives, and rocks. I heard someone shout and turned around to see one of the guards on the ground. Him and another had been bringing up the rear to watch our backs. The other one ran to help him up but it was obvious the fallen one wasn't going anywhere fast. A hatchet had struck the back of his leg at the knee. He shouted for his partner to leave him but the other guy refused. The mob was on top of them in a matter of seconds. The head guard told us not to stop. I guess Dorothy didn't want to see them suffer because she fired two of the largest fireballs I had seen her conjure directly at them. As the villagers flooded over them, the fireballs struck and exploded. The rest of us made it inside and locked the door behind us.

Chapter 6

Alice was tending to Glinda with healing spells to help her recover quicker. Eric and I responded to shouts in the main hall while the remaining guards barred the door and windows. Dorothy had ran ahead to light all the torches and candles but found trouble. Luckily, Adam was with her and whatever they encountered was dead by the time Eric and I showed up.

"The shadow creatures are susceptible to either light or magic or both," Adam told us when we came in. "My sword wasn't very effective until she cast a fire spell on it causing it to burn." His arm was bleeding from three scratches.

"You gonna make it?" I asked him.

"Probably not... Sorry I couldn't teach you everything I know before I leave this world."

Dorothy stepped next to him and said, "shall I call for Alice to patch you up?" His face began to get red and he developed a stutter.

"Hey, Alice, can you come here when you get the chance?" Eric called through the doorway.

"Hey, you're supposed to be the silent one!" Adam shouted. "Don't break character!" I think it was the exhaustion that caused us to laugh harder at this banter than we normally would have. We needed that, though. There hadn't been as much laughing lately.

The head guard came in and scolded us for goofing off. He told us that we had to get all the windows and any other entrances blocked off immediately. Glinda wanted to help us but was overcome with grief from losing two of our teammates. In her mind, it was her job to protect everyone and keep them safe and healthy. She hates violence and confrontation but has a strong devotion to everyone's well-being. It's not about her, it's always about everyone else. She pushes herself way too hard but I think that makes her stronger than any of us.

"Hey, Glinda," I said as I put an arm around her. "Why don't you go have a seat? We can handle this. You need to rest up."

"No, I can't," she said, choking up. "I have to make sure we're all okay. There's still too much danger and I can't lose anyone else." With that last sentence, she started crying. She covered her face with her hands and put herself into my chest while I hugged her. I looked over to see Eric in the doorway and I just shrugged because I knew he understood the situation since he had a protectionist mentality, too. He continued to stare for a moment, dropped his gaze, then met mine again and nodded before walking off. I wasn't sure what that was about but I assumed it was his acknowledgment to what was going on with Glinda. That he understood.

It wasn't long before we had everything blocked off. A couple of villagers broke through windows but since it was such a narrow space we were able to keep them at bay. It was the darkest part of the night, but for the time being, we were safe. I knew it wouldn't last but it was a nice reprieve.

As time passed, we swept through the building hoping to find anything and everything that we could use to defend ourselves. Eventually, we found a trapdoor that was hidden beneath the former mayor's desk. One of the guards checked it out and determined it might make for a safe way out but the head guard thought that a trap for us would be waiting at the other end so we left it alone.

A couples hours passed and it was becoming harder and harder to stay awake. "The sun should be rising soon, right?" Adam was peeking through a small separation between two boards that were up against a window. "A little longer than soon, but yes," the head guard told us. "Which means that they'll perform some sort of desperate maneuver before too long." Glinda and Alice had fallen soundly asleep. There were still tear marks down Glinda's cheeks.

Nearly another hour passed before the room shook and a loud crash rang through our ears. They had knocked open the front doors and were only a short hallway away from us. We turned to hop down the trapdoor when someone yelled for it. "Don't think I don't still own my memories of this place," the Mayor said from his chair. We had never even seen him take his position there. "We already have control of the secret passage," he said with a smile. Then possessed dogs on leashes were brought in behind us. We were surrounded.

"Here's the plan: you all have become strong inconveniences, so I am going to turn you into strong assets," the Mayor said, stepping down from his desk. I thought I heard Alice whisper something to Dorothy from behind me but I kept my eyes on the enemy.

"You will become leaders in my slave army as we conquer the region." The darkness began to flow from his hands. He was ready to make his first move when a small explosion rocked the ceiling above the doorway behind us.

Everyone looked up to see small amounts of rubble crumbling from overhead before turning their gaze to Dorothy. "Was that it?" the Mayor asked. "Your final effort at stopping me?"

"Yes!" Alice shouted as she used her magic to cause the fractured stones overhead to fall. The rest of the roof began caving in while the columns along the walls busted apart. Eric and Adam were already breaking open a window. Glinda sent a group of pixies out the window before us to create some light. As we landed outside, villagers that had been surrounding the building rushed us. We didn't hesitate to react violently this time. "This way!" the head guard shouted, beckoning us to the left. The exterior wall of the town hall collapsed into the street while the roof completely fell in. Glinda created more and more pixies before I urged her to hold back out of fear she would overexert herself again.

The moon and stars were still hidden so we couldn't know for sure what time it was but we believed the sun would be rising in about an hour. I hoped that it wasn't possible that the Mayor was powerful enough to block out the sun; if he was, he would have already killed or possessed us. So just one more hour. One more hour.

We didn't get very far down the road before the Mayor appeared in front of us in a burst of darkness. The girls all reacted out of reflex by firing a spell at him but he deflected all of them with a swing of his arm. His body was brimming with dark energy now. "I gave you a chance," he said as he powered up energy in his palms. "Now, I'm just going to kill you." Alice caused stones from the roadway to smack him from both sides as a distraction while Eric threw his spear, infused with magic to propel it faster. Dorothy lit the spear on fire before it could connect. Alice's distraction proved successful because the spear connected into his chest. Adam and I both charged the man. The two guards protected us from villagers to our rear.

Adam didn't want to take any chances so he threw one spinning sword as we closed in. The Mayor rallied quickly, though, and used dark magic to send both of us into walls on each side of the road. Then he pushed his magic harder and caused the two of us to fall through and into each building. Glinda sent two pixies to each of us since we were inside the darkness. The pixies provided light and weak healing magic. The warm light was enough to keep me from passing out. I pulled myself to my feet and peered through the hole in the wall to see Eric wrestling his spear free before the Mayor punched him straight into the ground. As soon as he was on the ground and out of the way, Dorothy had an opening to launch a huge fireball. Alice sent more stones flying at the Mayor to distract him. The fireball managed to connect with a loud explosion. I was pushed back to the ground from the blast. My face was actually hot from the heat of the fire.

I climbed back up and out of the wall in time to see the dust and smoke get blown away by a swirling bubble of darkness surrounding the Mayor. The fireball never hit it's target. The Mayor picked Eric up by the throat. Adam came up behind the villain, swinging a sword at his neck. I was on the other side, ready to stab his midsection. The Mayor didn't budge but he caused a pulse of dark energy to erupt from his body and send all three of us flying back. Alice caused a flurry of rocks to come at the Mayor from behind but he turned and caught them with his magic and sent them after all three girls. Glinda generated a quick barrier but it was so weak from not having time to charge that the rocks caused it to shatter. Some of them managed to hit their targets. Pixies were sent to us guys while Alice put a healing spell on herself and the girls.

This whole time, the two guards were fighting furiously to keep the villagers at bay. They had pixies surrounding them, casting simple healing spells that kept them going. There were bodies and pieces of dead villagers all over the place. The guards were covered in blood and sweat. They had both lost their own weapons in the fray and were using whatever they could get their hands on from the townspeople.

We were nearing the end of our ropes. Dorothy was too proud to show it, but she was exhausted. Glinda also hadn't fully recovered and the healing spells Alice had been casting were taking a toll on her.

The Mayor noticed the weakness in the girls and caught on that Glinda's instant-cast barriers were fragile. Six dagger-like creations of darkness appeared in the air around him. He sent two flying after each girl. Eric tried to jump in the way but wasn't able to. Adam dove after the Mayor at the moment he attacked. And I was too stunned to do anything. I just watched while Glinda tried to erect a defense. While Dorothy sent fireballs to stop them. While Alice pulled up a thin wall of stone. It all happened so fast, but also slow enough the I was able to see every detail of the events.

The daggers broke through every piece of defense and weren't even slightly distracted from their targets. I shouted something as they penetrated their obstacles and then I turned to attack the Mayor. His back was to me as he was picking up Adam over his head and hurling him back at the wall he had become familiar with earlier. The Mayor heard me shout and turned in time for me to land a punch in his face. I don't know how hard I hit him, or even if it did any kind of damage at all. I was so tired and felt so helpless so out of my rage I tried to put everything I had into my swing.

I had put my whole body into the punch and nearly fell forward. I couldn't see what was happening, though. I didn't even feel my fist touch his face. As I was about to connect, a bright light flashed from the end of my knuckles. It was so bright, like sunlight. I took a moment to register everything after swinging because I was unsure of what exactly happened. Then I realized my eyes were closed and I felt something in my hand. I wondered if I had swung my sword at his face instead of trying to punch. In the passion of my rage, I didn't know what had happened. I opened my eyes, looking down at my right hand, and found a most peculiar piece of craftsmanship.

Chapter 7

The Mayor was no longer in front of me, and the villagers fighting the guards had all collapsed to the ground. Everyone was staring at me, and I was staring at the object in my hand. It was a sword, but one unlike any I'd ever seen before. The blade was longer than my sword. It stretched about the length from my shoulder to my fingertips. And it looked white. Not shiny and silvery like every other sword, but shiny and pale white. The hilt was wrapped in white leather and was the length of about one-and-a-half hands. The end of the hilt was fastened with a sparkling gem that might've been a diamond. The guard was the only piece that wasn't white. It looked like golden feathers making up two wings. The most interesting thing about the entire piece, though, was that the blade seemed to glow. I thought it was coming from the light of the pixies reflecting off the white metal but it soon became very obvious in the dim light that the blade was indeed glowing on its own.

Nobody had anything to say. Everyone was as stunned in silence as I was. Well, except Adam, who found something explicit to blurt out. It wasn't until we heard one of the guards fall down that everyone snapped out of their trance. Glinda, frantic and apologetic that she hadn't noticed sooner, rushed to take care of the two. Only one of their pixies remained and was nearly faded out of existence like the others she'd cast for them. Alice joined Glinda to help in any way she could but the two men were badly injured and the girls were at their limit of exhaustion.

The rest of us postponed our investigation of the unusual turn of events to see to the guards. The head guard had been pierced in the ribs with a pitchfork and the other was barely breathing but wouldn't open his eyes. Glinda was pushing herself to delirium to fix them; the light coming from her hands was dimming as quickly as she could generate it. She was in tears when Eric finally grabbed her and took her aside. She pushed and fought back but he held firm. Alice remained but her magic pool was nearly empty so her healing spells were only good enough to numb the pain.

Dorothy knelt down next to the head guard. "Should we put you two out of your misery?" He coughed up a little bit of blood and said, "that'd probably be best. We wouldn't want to fall under the control of that beast." I stepped forward after she looked back at us. "Are you sure they won't make it?" Alice just looked up at me, shook her head, stood up, and walked back to console Glinda. Dorothy stood up and the head guard grabbed her ankle. "Just... don't use fire, okay?" She nodded and created a spike of ice in front of his forehead. Adam grabbed his hilt with both hands and aimed the tip of his blade at the other guard. They hesitated a moment, but did what they had to do.

We walked for maybe a block or two in silence. I honestly didn't know how far. It seemed to me like everyone was falling asleep on their feet. For some reason, though, I felt a little revitalized. My brain was exhausted but my body felt like it could continue fighting. The sword was still in my hand; I didn't know how to put it away since it wouldn't fit in my old scabbard. I brought along my old sword, just in case, but left it in its sheath. I couldn't fight with two like Adam. I quickly discovered that my new sword felt warm, not just to my hand, but to any part of my body it came close to. It was almost a comforting feeling.

Finally, Adam broke the silence by asking what I did to make it appear and where the Mayor went.

"I can't say for sure. I went to punch him in the face out of anger for attacking the girls the way he did last and then there was a bright light and then this is suddenly in my hand and the Mayor is gone. I was just so furious that the girls had been hurt... Wait a minute," I looked at the girls. "Why didn't any of you get hurt from his attack?"

"Simple," Dorothy began.

"The daggers never hit!" Alice cut in. We were puzzled.

"It must have something to do with the magic of your sword," Dorothy considered. "Maybe you killed him or injured him enough to break his control of the darkness. That would explain why all of his henchmen stopped."

We continued on, each person giving their own inputs from the results of the battle. Glinda remained silent, however. She wouldn't take her eyes off the ground. "Glinda," I said. She didn't look up. "Hey," I put a hand on her shoulder and everyone else stopped and came to us.

"I'm a failure," she said. She didn't start to cry this time.

"No you are absolutely not!" Alice said putting an arm around her.

"Yes, I am! My only job is to heal and protect and I haven't been even remotely successful with that tonight! I let all of our new companions die! They were husbands and brothers to our village and no they're gone and it's all my fault!" She pushed our arms away from her. I'd never seen her this angry. She was angry at herself for, what she believed, not trying hard enough. She continued to shout, and then stopped to pick up rocks and throw them at windows as she continued shouting. She described to us how she had always had the desire in her heart to help others and the one thing she was passionate about was something she apparently couldn't do. She thought herself useless to us and everyone. We kept trying to cut in and calm her down with the truth that she really is the most valuable person on our team.

"Glinda," Adam began. "You've saved me so many times… I would have died long ago if it wasn't for you. You're my angel."

"All of us would be dead if it wasn't for you. You are the purpose for and the source of our success," Eric said, grabbing her hand. She met his gaze with her own teary eyes and then wrapped her arms around him and began crying. It made the rest of us sad to see her like this. She was so strong and took such good care of us. She really was like the bedrock that kept us stable. It was hard to see her break. I was reminded of the time I secretly caught my mother breaking down on the floor over my father. The emotions flooded in and I just wanted to cry, too.

Her despair was affecting the rest of the party. We were all exhausted on many levels and distraught over the loss of half our team. Being as tired as I'd ever been was beginning to affect my own feelings. Being this tired was putting me in an "I don't care" kind of mood. I noticed that I didn't feel as bad about the guards' deaths as I should have and that all I really wanted to do was lay down. I tried to convince myself that I'm just exhausted and that I really do feel grief. I was pondering my own emotions and looking at the sky when I noticed something that shouldn't be. "Hey, guys," I said. "Look." Their eyes followed my finger to a blank sky.

"Wait, shouldn't the moon and stars be out now that the Mayor is dead?" Adam asked.

"This night is becoming curiouser and curiouser!" Alice exclaimed. I felt a chill run down my spine and gulped. Apparently, we weren't finished yet.

We made it to the town gate that we first entered to find it shut. "This can't be happening," Alice said, putting her hands on her head.

"I'm too drained to go another round," Dorothy announced as she look at her hands. "I might have to resort to my fists." She gently punched Eric's chest.

"Those exercises we used to do might finally get put to use!"

"Let's hope not," he replied.

"It's gonna be alright," I said trying to calm them. "We'll just climb up the guard tower and open it. For all we know, they shut it earlier."

Adam went ahead into the tower. We waited for a few minutes, assuming that his pace up the steps could be slowed from fatigue and maybe the process to raise the gate was a little confusing. We sat mostly in silence on a bench, too tired to speak. After some minutes passed the gate remained closed but Adam came bolting out of the tower with a cloud of darkness chasing him. Dorothy let loose a tiny little fireball, much smaller than usual, that hit the target directly and caused it to dissipate.

I asked him what happened and he explained to us that he was trying to work the lever to raise the gate when that cloud attacked him. He then showed us cut marks on his arms and neck. Glinda had a pixie patch him right up since they were such light injuries.

The cloud reformed in a swirl some distance down the road. The Mayor stepped out from the cloud looking as if he hadn't ever been in a confrontation before. We were stunned. After all we did, after the light caused him to disappear, after four of our companions died in front of us, he was perfectly fine! How could that be?!

"Pardon my absence," he said, taking off his glasses and polishing them with a handkerchief. "The light from before surprised me so I had to take a moment to gather myself before we could complete our business." He put his glasses back on and gave us the same toothy smile as before. His body began to radiate with dark energy again but it felt different this time. His energy seemed a weight to the air. It was as if the gravity was increasing above us. Our group was already very weary so this new weight affected us more than it probably should have. I could feel the pressure in my head expanding, but my body felt as strong as ever. I knew that if something was going to happen, my new weapon would have to be the driving force.

The rest of the group was slow to mobilize, but I didn't wait. I stepped forward with my sword ready and glowing in obvious opposition of his power. He accepted my challenge and fired a missile of black energy at my heart. I batted it with my sword, causing it to explode. He was already creating more as I retaliated and then sent six flying towards me from different directions. I didn't know what to do with my new sword besides swing it around. I began to feel a tinge of doubt in myself. Then, all the projectiles exploded. I turned to see Dorothy, Alice, and Glinda standing with a hands up. Dorothy just nodded at me. I nodded back while Eric and Adam ran past me. They were almost completely drained of energy, but we were still in this together.

The battle that followed was longer than it should've been for our current levels of stamina. The girl's distracted the Mayor from a distance and stopped his missiles whenever they could. The other two guys created diversions up close and took strong hits from the enemy. They were sacrificing themselves for me to have an opening. Every connection of my sword to his body was shown on his face. The guys noticed that and we knew that it would come down to me to ultimately stop this guy once and for all.

Glinda was relying on her pixies to keep everyone healed. Her pool of magic was nearly dry and her upset emotions were having an obvious negative effect on her performance. The Mayor had been annoyed by the floating lights and was taking every chance he got to shoot one down. We originally had one pixie floating around each of us but as the battle ensued we were down to three.

Our foe was also taking advantage of any lull between our melee assaults to send a shadowy dart flying towards the girls. Glinda was the main target so Alice and Dorothy had to keep an eye on her as well as themselves. As the fighting raged on, us guys on the front line were tiring out at an exponential rate since we had to move around him so much. I noticed the others were slowing down quicker than I was.

This deceleration in our attacks gave the Mayor more and more opportunities to fire at the girls which in turn caused them to defend themselves instead of distract him with their spells. He was quickly getting the upper-hand and he knew it. But my sword still damaged him and I could tell he was making special note of my every movement whenever he could.

When I cut him for the third time, he roared in anger and caused a thick cloud of dark mist to swing around his body and hit me in the gut, sending me up into the air and crashing me back to the ground. It was still pushing me into the road when a pixie cut back and forth through it to separate it from his control. Then the pixie made the mistake of turning to me and cast a small healing spell. The Mayor floated behind it on the cloud of smoke that had become his feet and grabbed the pixie with his right hand and crushed it into sparkling dust. Eric then came up behind him with a flaming spear and stabbed him in the back. The Mayor seemed unaffected and swung his arm at Eric's head who managed to duck while Adam came from the other side with both swords aimed at a pair of legs.

Their efforts gave me enough time to get to my feet. Out of anger at watching the pixie be murdered so brutally, I swung my sword as hard as I could. I guess my emotions were a factor in my abilities because me sword glowed brightly as I brought it towards my target. The blade made a flash as it cut through the Mayor. He screamed in agony and made a blast wave of darkness erupt from his body. The other guys flew backwards but I barely budged. This time I tried to stab him but he jumped back too far for my blade to connect. The magic of my sword made up for the gap by firing a spike of light from the tip and through his midsection.

He fell to one knee, clutching his belly with both arms. He looked up just in time to see a blast of green magic come from his right and a fireball come from his left. The two met in an explosion at his head. He was facedown and motionless after that.

The guys and I slowly approached him to finish the job as he struggled push himself up. He was mumbling something and I didn't hear most of it but I think he was asking some kind of queen for more strength. "You guys get any of that?" I asked. Then, his body floated up and righted itself. He was suspended in the air as high as a person and looking at the sky. Then, smoke started spiraling around his whole body. He began laughed and thanking someone. "Phillip, get this over with!" Adam shouted. I didn't really think about my next move but I knew I wanted to hit him and hit him hard. The attack just came to me after seeing it performed so many times. I threw my sword and the magic of it caused it to spin like a wheel of light energy creating a dazzling display with sparkles flying everywhere. The attack hit it's target with a bright flash and the Mayor fell to the ground as my sword kept going. I thought to myself that I wanted it back and told even told it to return. It kept going from a moment and then it flashed out of existence and then reappeared in my right hand in a glimmer of light and sparkles.

We all stood and watched as the body of the Mayor dissipated into nothingness. "Look!" Alice said hopping and pointing at the sky. Beyond the borders of the town, we saw a bright blue sky. The sun was rising. We looked around to see the blackness fade away to reveal a falling moon in the other direction and a handful of stubborn little stars still twinkling against the brightening blue background. We could finally sigh with relief. Before that, though, I couldn't hold back a laugh. I had to lean forward on my knees to laugh. Everyone else joined in with a chuckle or a giggle. We were alive and so, so, so very tired and that, to us, was hilarious.

Chapter 8

We were half a day late making it back home. A search party ran into us along the road in the forest and escorted us the rest of the way to the town hall. The main reason behind our tardiness was that we all slept in the nearest building after our last fight with the Mayor. We were so tired that we slept soundly on the floor with almost no form of cushion whatsoever and it was one of the deepest sleeps I have ever experienced.

Our mayor was less than pleased to see us report in so late, especially due to sleeping, and without our own personal guards. Once he heard our testimony, however, his anger disappeared. "It's a miracle you're all still alive," he said. "We are going to have to honor the lives and memories of the men who sacrificed themselves to save you kids and this town." After being released to our families, I proceeded to head straight for my bed. I didn't see the others for two days and found out that we all spent our time pretty much just sleeping and recovering.

Mother was crying when she saw me. She hugged me as if she had never hugged me before and I did the same in return. I felt so bad to worry her this much because of what dad had done to her. I didn't want to follow in his footsteps of upsetting this family over and over again; I knew I needed to be better than that. After sleeping away most of my first day home, I woke up late in the evening only to lie in bed for a while thinking about the impact my latest exploits had had on my family. I couldn't help but wonder what it would be like if I died. I started to reconsider my adventurous habits and ponder a quiet future here in my village. An easy future, one where I stay close to my family and raise one of my own. Mother would be so happy to see me everyday and I could help her around the house whenever she grew old. I would have so few worries and with no threats of danger I could live in peace and harmony with a wife and kids.

Images of having everyone together for big family gatherings and special family events continued to flash through my mind. It would be such a lovely, calm future to have. Then I couldn't help but wonder if I would be happy with it. Everyone else in the pictures my mind produced were happy and laughing, but my smile seemed fake. Was that a future that is right for me or is it right for everyone else? *No,* I thought to myself. *I don't think I could live with it. Not happily, at least.* My passion is exploration and discovery. I enjoyed seeing and learning and experiencing new things. Truly, I didn't think I could stay in my hometown forever. I knew that I couldn't and I had known that for a while. I got to thinking that it kind of sucks. I could have such an easy, carefree life at home... but I knew that I wouldn't be happy. It was as if I was destined for something more, far beyond the borders of this community.

Adam showed up at the house after a couple relaxing days. I was chopping firewood when he arrived with a bag of food from the market.

"Did you get the news?" he asked me.

"No," I said, "what news? Something happen?"

"We have a meeting with the mayor at sunset. Not sure what it's about, though." We chatted for a little longer and then he went home to help cook dinner. Sunset was only a few hours away so I had time to finish up some work, eat, get anxious, and head on over there for whatever mysterious meeting is awaiting us.

I ran into Eric and Dorothy on my way over and asked if they had any idea what this was all about.

"Not a clue," Dorothy said. "But I'll bet you it's another assignment."

"You think so?" I asked and then Eric said, "they already debriefed us on our last mission, so it could only be another." I think I kind of expected it to be another quest, but I would also be a little surprised if our parents were even slightly okay with the idea.

Sure enough, Dorothy was right. "We need you to make another delivery, this time to Alican," the mayor said, holding up a not and handing it out for me to grab.

"Alican? Isn't that a port city?" Alice asked.

"Yes," the mayor replied. "It is directly south. You'll run into a main road and plenty of signs that will take you directly there."

"I've heard it's a beautiful place," Glinda said excitedly. The mayor informed us of our mission which was pretty much the same as the last only that we will be on our own this time. The mayor of Alican will have another assignment for us after we make our delivery so we weren't given a return time which made this quest seem more real, more dangerous, and maybe even a little more exciting.

The reason for the sunset meeting was so we could go straight home, get some rest, and leave the next morning. Alican was about a day, day-and-a-half longer of a journey that our last one but it was more or less much easier to get to than Castelle. Mother was crying when I arrived home. She hugged me and we talked for a while. Apparently, the Mayor had met with all of our parents the day before and explained the details of our upcoming journey. None of them were okay with it, but he convinced him the importance of the mission and that we were capable, more than any of the guards, of completing the tasks asked of us. Mother told me how proud she was of my accomplishments through her tears and made me promise to return to her in one piece. I thought about dad again and how much pain he had caused her. I didn't hesitate to make the promise she asked of me. No matter what happens, I will return and make her so happy. Happier than anyone ever could. I told her how much I loved her and then went to get my things ready before bed.

I didn't get nearly as much sleep as I'd have liked. The anxiety caused from this upcoming mission and the emotional state my mother was in put me in a weird mood. I tossed and turned for what felt like hours, just thinking about stuff. Every so often, I would stop myself mid-thought and tell myself to try and fall asleep. I would even focus on nothing but blackness to hopefully shut my brain off but the darkness in my mind brought images of the living shadows I had encountered and their eyes watching me. Before long, I began to see eyes staring at me from the corners of my room. I eventually fell asleep from exhaustion and didn't even dream.

A guard came to the house about an hour after sunrise. He informed me that the team is to depart from the south gate in an hour. I took a little time to get out of bed. It wasn't that I didn't want to go on another adventure because I was sure that did, but my body just felt heavy. I don't know if adventuring was becoming like a chore or if it was the fact that it was like a job now. Or maybe both of those are becoming my reality. I stayed in bed, staring at the ceiling, and realizing that these quests for our mayor was different than what I had been doing in the past. Before, my friends and I had all the freedom to make our own decisions, but now we had missions and that made it feel more like work than an exciting journey. I tried to convince myself that it still could be seen as one but it was just a different feeling to be exploring for a job rather than the sheer thrill of adventure. Mom finally snapped me out of my trance with breakfast so I decided to leave those thoughts for another day. It was time to get to work.

I made it to the southern entrance of town a little early. I didn't want to stick around the house and drag on a goodbye. I assured everyone that I would be home soon enough and with gifts from the big city. My younger siblings were excited about that. When I arrived, Alice and Adam were already there waiting. They were playing some game with their hands where one person tries to slap the other's hands before they can pull them away. Alice was giggling because Adam wasn't letting her get ready first before he slapped her hands. "Sorry," I said. "I hope I'm not interrupting." They both perked up as if trying to hide something. "Where's that fancy sword of yours?" Adam asked. I held out my right hand and made it appear in a flash of light and sparkles. I explained how I spent some time playing around with it to try and understand it as best as possible but it was still pretty new and mysterious. No matter how much I experimented with it, I still felt like there was more to learn but I couldn't find ways to unlock anything more. "Maybe it really is tied to your emotions," Dorothy said from behind. Her, Eric, and Glinda were walking toward us. "So that just means we have to nearly kill you and then we'll see more tricks, right?" Adam asked, partially unsheathing a sword. We laughed as I dared him to try it.

The guards at the gate wished us the best of luck as we departed. The two of them each had a bag of supplies for us, as per the mayor's orders. None of it was anything really special, but enough useful stuff to at least last us a week. If we were careful, we could make it all the way to Alican without having to hunt or fish.

It was about four boring days of walking along a wide, dirt path before we made it to the highway. It was the first time any of us had ever seen a highway and it must've been obvious on our faces. A road at least twice as wide as any I had ever seen before and made up entirely of tan-colored bricks. People of every variety dotted the road as far as the eye could see. Along the road were mile markers, signposts to indicate directions and where other pathways led, and countless vendors with their carts. We came onto the highway southeast of another, fairly large city known as Albaeta, and approximately four days from Alican which meant there were plenty of people to be found.

Eric made a pretty good suggestion during our first night along the highway. As we started to get settled by some trees along the road, I noticed him standing and looking all around us. I asked him what was wrong while I unrolled my bed furs. "With so many people around, wouldn't it be a better idea to move a little farther off the road," he started. "And also have someone keep watch." I looked behind us as the landscape to find nothing but small, rolling hills, some trees, and bushes. It seemed safe enough and I agreed to his idea to move farther away. On one hand, the road was safe from animals and other creatures because of the constant activity and lights, but there was also the threat of thieves. We saw quite a number of people sleeping along the road and no sort of criminal activity, but it was better to be safe than sorry.

We didn't get much farther off the road before Adam spoke up with an idea of his own. "Hey, since we have to keep watch, that'll only give each of us five hours of sleep. We can't do two hours each because that would total up to be an unnecessary amount of time. How about we keep going a little longer and get our sleep through the darkest parts of the night so we're finishing up our rest closer to sunrise." It was an interesting thought. On our way here, we hadn't had a need for keeping watch. Dorothy had been setting up small fireballs to keep the animals at bay and Glinda let loose a couple pixies to alert her if anything came too close. If we tried to do that now, right off the highway, some people may see the lights and want to join us, or ask for something, or share a meal, or whatever else. We all discussed Adam's proposal and eventually came to a unanimous agreement to keep going a little while longer.

This pretty much stayed our routine for the next few days up until we reached the city. We mingled as little as possible with other travelers but meeting strange people and merchants was inevitable. Fortunately, the only creatures we found along the way were pets or farm animals. The long walks were, for the most part, boring, but it was kind of nice not to get into a fight each day. I could tell that Adam was getting anxious, though. I also think Dorothy might have been, as well, because she sometimes seemed a little agitated and was more short with us than usual. Alice, Eric, and I enjoyed some action, but those two hotheads made up the tip of our spear.

Chapter 9

The view I woke up to was beyond anything I'd seen before, comparable only to being in the mountains and looking across the vast landscape beyond. Our mayor had stashed a little bit of money in with our supplies and we earned even more from making our delivery so we were able to afford two fairly luxurious rooms at an inn near the water. The window by my bed was as big as a wall at my house back in Valencia. I was awoken by the sound of seagulls and the salty sea wind coming in through the window that must've been opened while I slept. It had to have been Eric because he usually wakes up early and Adam was sprawled out all over his bed with a sheet wrapped around one leg and two pillows on the floor. I got up and admired the view from our room once more before going to eat breakfast. As I got myself ready to move, I could see the harbor and hear people hustling and bustling on the cobblestone street three floors below. The noise put me at ease. It made me feel safe.

I met Eric, Glinda, and Dorothy in the dining room on the first floor. I say dining room, but it was more like a fancy restaurant. It had people servicing the tables but there was also something called a buffet where we could go up and get our own food from a selection mostly of foods I had never seen or heard of before. This entire city was full of new experiences. We sat and chatted while we tried all the different foods and drinks available. There was still nearly an hour before our guide was to arrive and show us major parts of the city. The mayor we had met the day before assigned us a person to, in her words, "keep us from getting lost or into trouble" while she prepared our next assignment. We were given all of today to explore and relax. I was surprised that she didn't immediately have anything for us to do but the guide informed us last night that she was an extremely busy woman and the contents of our next mission couldn't be completed until she received our delivery.

I cannot begin to describe the beauty of Alican. The architecture was like nothing I had ever seen before; mostly made from stone with statues and artwork carved into it. The guide gave us history lessons about the whole city and some individual, significant parts of it. Alican was one of the oldest cities in the country and the harbor actually was the oldest and the second-largest next to the one at the capital.

We visited two cathedrals and even went to the top of the bell tower at one. We visited the harbor where the second-largest largest market in the entire country resided. It was crowded and stressful to navigate so the guide took us to a bridge that overlooked the market and we watched the people move about. Everyone was dressed differently and acted much stranger than we were accustomed to. The guide told us that the only way to survive in a city like this is to be assertive and always watch our surroundings because thieves and the desperate poor knew to target visitors. He then took us to the naval base nearby and we spent a significant time there admiring the ships and watching the uniformed soldiers conduct their work. Before we left there we were given an escort aboard the king's ship that he had stationed there for his trips to the southeastern countries.

This city was like a completely different planet to us and every bit of it was amazing. By the time we made it to dinner at the nicest restaurant in the city I was contemplating not returning home until I had seen all of the country. My friends and I even discussed that thought and we shared laughs along with our hunger for more adventures. It's so interesting how a little bit of traveling and having new experiences abroad like this makes you desire more and more. We had always experienced an increased thirst for more journeys after returning home but none of us had felt it like this before.

We reported in that the town hall at noon and were taken into the smallest of the meeting rooms and placed at a table that could comfortably seat approximately twenty-two people. A full fireplace nearly as big as the window in our room at the inn crackled behind the head seat. Windows along the wall behind us stretched from the floor to the ceiling and looked out over a park that was as large as one of the farm fields back home. The mayor came in a few minutes after us and was followed by her assistant who was struggling to carry a huge stack of papers.

The mayor first told us how busy she was today so she got right down to business. "We have been aware of this threat of darkness for quite some time now," she began. "Our guards here are well-trained to combat the creatures we have found so far and the number of travelers and adventurers that have passed through here have proven to be valuable assets. We are okay here and do not need your assistance, but another city does." Her assistant pulled out three maps of the region and we paired up to look at them while the assistant walked behind us, pointing out what the mayor was talking about. "The next largest city to our southwest, Ruciam, is under attack. It is located on the Egura river in a valley surrounded by hills and small mountains. We believe that there is some sort of leadership in the surrounding area that is watching the city and coordinating troops. The city cannot spare the manpower anymore to seek out the source of the enemy and they have requested our aid. That is where you come in." She gave us a moment to register all the information and then took our questions. We didn't have many and she couldn't completely answer any we did have since there was so little information to begin with.

After our discussion she handed us two sealed letters to be delivered to the mayor of Ruciam upon our arrival. "You will be given a boat to take you down the river right to the city. You are expected to arrive in two days."

"I'm sorry," I said. "Expected?"

"Yes," the mayor responded with a serious look on her face. "I told their mayor before you arrived here that we will be sending your team." We all looked at her in bewilderment. What initiative! I had to admire this mayor. She was at least as smart and strong as any grown man I had met before and didn't even look quite as old as the council members back home. I guess one would have to be highly capable to run such a vast and busy city. I wanted to ask more questions about her but she excused herself to attend to other matters. As her assistant gathered the stack of papers together she apologized for the short meeting and told us that since the mayor was also the head of the judiciary committee in the city she had little time to spare anyone. I took another moment to be impressed before we left the room.

We were escorted back to the entrance of the building where we met our guide again. He took us to another restaurant on the other side of the park and we were seated on the roof of the building. Birds joined us at our table and Adam was scolded by the restaurant staff for feeding them. Our guide ordered us the best wine from the menu and then discussed the course of events from this point on. He will take us back to our inn and then leave us. We have complete freedom until twilight when he will pick us up and take us to our boat.

He also said that if we did any kind of shopping then we are allowed to leave all of the extra stuff here and they will store it for us until we return or they can ship it home. Glinda and Alice were excited to splurge on clothes while Eric, Adam, and I were more interested in the blacksmith shops we passed before. The guide showed the girls where the two best shopping districts were on the map and where the best blacksmiths were for us. We were on a semi-tight budget so he told us which places were most affordable. Dorothy was the only one left out. Alice asked if she wanted to join her and Glinda but she said she had something else in mind to fill the free time.

The girls went down a street to the north of the inn where most of the clothing stores were. Us guys went to two blacksmith shops along the waterfront. The road we took had one of the best views of the water and connected two harbor markets. We didn't go too far south along the road because our guide warned us of the southern and southeastern part of town where there was a higher crime rate.

The first shop we found had some pretty good prices but we wanted to find the best bargain so we went to the other one only to find higher prices for nearly the same stuff so we went back. I found two weapons I really liked but I remembered the new sword I just got so I refrained from making any weapon purchases. I was a little discouraged until a fancy leather vest that had pockets on it and was thick enough to protect my midsection better than the average outfit. The salesman also talked each of us into buying shirts made of tiny metal rings to provide the "best weight-to-protection ratio money could buy!" Adam traded in his two swords to get a discount on two new ones while Eric struggled to choose between two spears. One was a little longer than his current one and made of the same material but the other one was stronger and more durable. He opted for the latter and we finally left looking and feeling better.

Alice and Glinda were sitting outside the inn on the patio and drinking tea whenever we made it back. "Oh! Look at these hotties!" Alice shouted uncomfortably loud. Glinda just giggled while Alice said, "we're waiting on our friends but you boys are free to entertain us until they arrive." Then she winked at us.

Adam sat down next to her and said, "thanks, man. We need something to do while we wait for the brothel to open up."

"MAN?!" Alice pushed him out of his chair and said, "hope you like hot tea!" and splashed her drink on his face. Adam started screaming before the liquid even touched his face and then realized the tea wasn't actually hot. The two carried on with their bickering while Glinda told us about all the pretty outfits they bought and showed off her new wand and Alice's new staff. The staff was quite impressive. Alice had never actually used a weapon before but this one had been carved from an ancient tree and blessed by some old druid so it would help amplify her nature powers. Glinda's wand offered a similar effect in that she could easily channel magic through it.

Dorothy finally joined us about a half hour later while we sipped on our tea. She was carrying two new books so we didn't hesitate to ask her a load of questions about her afternoon. As usual, she didn't feel the need to say much but did mention visiting a magic shop and bookstore. She had apparently read through as many spells as she could and even copied some down into the notes pages of the two books she bought.

"Isn't that like stealing?" Glinda asked.

"Yes," Dorothy replied, and then took a sip of the drink in front of her.

"I'm excited to see what you've learned!" Alice said and asked if she wanted to get a wand while in town.

"I don't like wands," she replied. "They impair my casting. I like to have the freedom of my fingers while I weave my spells." Glinda and Alice both seemed to understand. Us guys didn't have a clue of what they began discussing. Magic was a whole different world to us. We each could harness a tiny bit to add a little more bite to our physical attacks but that was about it. With my new sword, though, I guess I'd have to start learning a little more about magic so I tried to listen up but it was as if they were speaking another language half the time.

Our guide met us an hour later with a handful of city guards. Two of the guards gathered up the extra stuff that the girls bought and took them away to be shipped back to Valencia. The dock we were going to was on the southeastern side of town at the source of the Egura river where there was more criminal activity which is why we were given an armed escort. All the supplies we needed were already in our boat which also came with a few sailors to crew and navigate for us. It was a fairly small boat but much larger than any we had back home. I was more than excited to travel by water; it was something I had never done before. Back home, we have a decent number of fishing boats but all of them were used throughout the day for work. This was a whole new chapter in my book of adventures.

Chapter 10

"Pull! Hurry!" Eric shouted. Glinda did as she was told and then we all watched as a fish flew through the air and landed on the deck of the boat. He had been teaching her and Alice how to fish since he had the childhood experience of working with his father who did the job professionally.

In the past few hours, they had listened to every word he said and had caught a grand total of one fish. Dorothy chose not to take part and instead was under some shady umbrella reading one of her books. I figured she should be nearly done with it by now since that's pretty much all she'd done since we set off yesterday.

Adam and I passed our time by sparring a little bit with our new weapons. I was trying to get the hang of my new sword and he wasn't making it easy on me. His new swords were lighter but made of a stronger metal than the weapons he was used to so he was quicker and more deadly. It was pretty good training on my end but I got the feeling he was really pushing himself hard to get a decent workout in for himself.

Later that evening, the girls hadn't had much more luck with catching fish. Dorothy finally got tired of Alice's complaining so she handed her one of the books she bought and told her to check the notes in the back. Alice did and discovered that Dorothy had copied down some spells from a Druid's manual that she had found. "This is amazing, Dorothy!" Alice said excitedly. "But why didn't you just buy me the whole book?"
"I didn't feel like spending the money," she replied before going back to the front of the boat to practice her own incantations. After that we kind of lost Alice to the book for the rest of our time there.

The water had been good to us by this point so we were forecasted to arrive early. It was mid-morning on our second day and we were only a few hours out. I was pacing across the deck, admiring the sights, when I noticed Alice and Glinda back in their fishing spot. I didn't see any fishing poles so I decided to investigate. I approached in time to see a fish burst from the water and flop around in the air for a moment before returning beneath the waves. The girls then squealed and I covered my ears until they stopped. "What's going on?" I asked. "She can control the fish!" Glinda screamed. I was confused as to what she meant by 'control' so Alice demonstrated her new power once again. This time, three fish jumped back and forth through the air. "The notes

Dorothy wrote mostly focused on animal control," Alice explained. "I can use my nature magic to temporarily operate the mind and body of any animal." I was rather astounded but she clarified that it was an easy spell to produce but difficult to sustain and she would need a lot of practice with small animals before moving to larger beasts.

I decided to visit Dorothy at the back of the boat to ask her if she had learned anything new, as well. "Hey, Dorothy, what's up?" I asked her before she turned around abruptly and thrust out her palm at me. I saw a flash of purple and then a strange feeling came over me. I tried to move my arms and legs but they felt heavy, as if they were being pulled in the opposite of whatever direction I tried to move them. I wanted to shout at Dorothy but the words were slow to come out and even my throat felt heavy. Dorothy's palm was still out facing me but only for a moment then she flicked her wrist and pulled her hand away. I felt normal again.

"What the hell did you do to me?!"

"I was testing a new spell and needed a subject," she said matter-of-factly. "You just happened to be in the right place at the right time and performed perfectly."

She went back to looking through her book again while she explained to me the spell she just cast. "It's a spell called Despair and it slows a target for a given amount of time. The only downside right now is that I'm not strong enough to leave it to that amount of time; I have to maintain the spell for it to remain in effect." I was once again fascinated with my teammate. I then decided to visit the guys below deck and see what they were up to.

I could hear grunting and cursing before I even got to the room. The two were in there wrestling and throwing each other around. They had wrapped their fists in cloth to safely throw punches at each other's bodies. "Hey, Phillip, check out what Eric just taught me," Adam said approaching me. As quickly as I could register his words I found myself flying through the air and landing on my back. "You always had a slight advantage over me because you're a little taller but Eric showed me how to compensate." Some of the wind had been knocked out of me so I was coughing as I climbed to my feet. The two then proceeded to finish their match. I guess everyone was taking the free time to learn new things so I went back to talk to Glinda since she was the only one, besides me, who wasn't testing skills.

Back up on the deck, Glinda was dancing around with her new wand while Alice watched. At first, I thought she was dancing just for the sake of dancing but they I realized she was actually casting a flurry of spells. There were at least a dozen pixies floating around her at different distances and she was using each of them as a target. Flashes of light and sparkles were shimmering all across the deck as she continued to dance around ever so elegantly. I had never seen anyone dance in such a way before but then I remembered her briefly mentioning to me once before that she had been trained in the art of dancing for years as a little girl. I had never seen it put into action before but it explained why she had always been so dexterous and agile in combat. With all the lights dancing around alongside her, she almost resembled an angel.

After watching her for a while, I noticed that the spells she cast were brighter and more prominent than I remembered. In the past, her light spells and glows were mostly transparent and not bright enough to really irritate anyone. Now, everything shined much more distinctly and I had to squint my eyes at times. I guess I really was the only person on this vessel that wasn't improving. I might as well have not gotten a new weapon after all.

I found an unoccupied railing along the side of the boat and sat down to watch the water. I got to thinking about all the improvements and training that my teammates were undergoing and why I wasn't doing the same thing. *Why can't I just get up and train, too*? I asked myself. Dorothy was so good at training alone but I felt like I needed a partner to work with. I sat and watched the waves batter the side of the boat for an unknown amount of time while I let the waves of my thoughts batter my emotions. *They're getting so strong and I'm getting left behind*, I said to myself. I was sure that if I stood up and materialized my sword, I could find something to do to get a workout in but I just couldn't make myself move. Self-doubt was piling up so I just decided to stay seated for a little while longer.

We could see the city on the horizon long before we arrived. The buildings of were tall and skinny compared to those of Alican. As we got closer it became more apparent that the entire town was floating on the water. The river split around the entire city to provide a first line of defence while walls stood right behind. This quest was becoming one amazing sight after another and all of it only exacerbated my hunger to see the rest of the world.

It appeared as if the entire city was made of wood. According to the sailor piloting our ship, this entire valley was once a forest but when we looked around in every direction, there wasn't a single tree to be found. As the city grew, the forests shrunk until all that was left were rolling fields, high towers, and thick walls.

The dock we pulled into was about as large as the harbor we left from and supposedly there was another one equal in size at the other end of the city. I tried not to be too surprised when I looked up at the buildings and realized how much taller they were up close. We had to tilt our heads back to see the tops of them. Back in Alican, the highest buildings reached only three floors while the church towers went higher.

Here, all the buildings were at least three floors with some reaching five or six. It only made sense, though, when we realized that every floor was only one or two rooms so they all ended up having about the same floor space as any other building, but it was still a sight to behold. The other impressive thing about the city was the smell. An assortment of new and disgusting smells combined together to make something that caused my nostrils to nearly bleed. We all began holding our noses out of reflex as we neared the city and the sailor assured us that we wouldn't ever get used to it.

A soldier of the city wearing black and brown leather and wielding a spear that had three points at the end greeted us as we docked. He welcomed us to the city and informed us that he will escort us to the town hall for a meal with the mayor while the contents of our next assignment were discussed. It was more than an hour past noon and hadn't eaten since right after sunrise which meant we were all pretty hungry so the news of a meal excited us but none of us were sure if we could eat with the putrid stench hovering about. The soldier laughed when Alice told him that and he clarified that the city smell is masked in most buildings. He also said we would eventually get used to it but I knew for sure that I didn't want to stay here long enough for that.

If it hadn't been for the smell, our walk to the town hall would've been a fun sightseeing experience. The entire city really did seem to be floating on the water. Roads had been replaced with bridges and canals and every building rested on a mini island of wood that came with at least one tiny little dock. I had to keep stretching my neck every so often to keep it from getting sore since I had it tilted back to look up at the tall buildings almost the whole walk.

The town hall was the only building in the city that was built differently. It was only two floors high and had the largest surface area of any building in the city. It was also the only structure made of stone. A wooden dock surrounded the massive stone base while thick columns reached up out of the water and supported the roof. It looked much like a temple and was surprisingly sturdy for being on the water. I expected it to shift when we climbed the stairs but it never budged so I could only assume this stone reached all the way to the floor of the lake. It was later that we found out that none of the buildings floated on the water here and that thick wooden (or in this building's case, stone) supports really did reach to the bottom of the lake.

The inside of the building was much more immaculate than we thought it would be. Apparently, the city generates quite a bit of money compared to the simple cost of living so many people live quite comfortably which, in turn, allows for a substantial tax rate.

The mayor was quite fat and carried a red tint to his face that matched his hair color. The selection that was already placed on the table for us to choose from was made up almost entirely of fish and strange plants that were grown in the water. I looked around the table to see a lot of puzzled or nauseous-looking faces from my teammates as they mulled over whatever was in front of them. None of us really ate much but the mayor made sure to get his fill while he spoke to us. Two servants stood by his sides to wipe his mouth, chin, and neck for him after some of his juicier cuisines and to refill his wine glass.

We were dismissed back to our inn after lunch and Dorothy asked our new guide if there was any place in town that didn't serve fish. He chuckled and took us to a tourist restaurant that specialized in a variety of 'foreign' foods. We stayed for quite a while trying out all the different variations of chicken and pork. When we finally left I felt like I had gained ten pounds and all I wanted was a nap.

A knock on the door woke us up around sunset. Even Eric was still asleep which means he ate as well as I did. A soldier was making sure we would be ready to go by dusk. According to the mayor, the creatures attack every night at different times. This first night we are supposed to meet with a captain of the night watch and assess the threat ourselves. Before sunrise we will be sent back to the inn for rest and around noon we will set out on horseback to find who or whatever is leading these creatures.

About an hour later we were ready and waiting outside the inn when a soldier showed up to escort us to one of the guard towers. There were a number of them that dotted the city and among the walls lining the lake but we were taken to a large tower near the southwestern harbor where we met a captain who appeared to me nearly fifty-years-old and looked quite tired. He informed us that the attacks have kept a general pattern and he had been busy since last night preparing for the oncoming assault. It was expected to be the largest yet. We asked how he could know that unless they had a hostage so he explained the pattern. "We get attacked every night," he began. "Every fifth night it has been a big assault and each big assault has been bigger than before. The last one proved to be more than we could handle so we predict this one to be particularly devastating which is why we needed you here." He then asked each of us what our abilities were so he could split us into two groups properly. "I'm sorry sir, but we work best as one unit," I said to him. My comment angered him and he shouted to me how he knew what was best for his city. He then split us up and sent us off to our positions.

Eric, Glinda, and Dorothy were assigned the southern edge of town while Alice, Adam, and I were stationed to the northwest end only a series of blocks north of where the captain's tower was. We met up with a young lieutenant who was to be in charge of us for the night. He seemed to be in his mid-twenties and quite muscular. Alice was smitten almost immediately and told us how attractive she thought he was which lead to Adam badmouthing him for the remainder of the night and sparked a slight, one-sided rivalry.

Our first order was to get torches lit. A lot of torches. I lost count of how many we lit and placed in metal holders all over our zone. The people who resided in the buildings around the city joined in by hanging torches outside their windows. I was coming down from a scaffold along the city wall when I looked across town. It looked like the stars of the sky had fallen onto the city. Thousands of twinkling fires covered nearly every inch of the town. It was beautiful.

We were among a platoon of about forty soldiers. Some of them, I noticed, were as young as us or even younger. To have recruits this young meant that they either needed all the help they could get to stem this threat or that they had suffered considerable losses over the weeks. Or both.

It hadn't gotten very dark before the first attack happened. It came from the south side of town. We heard some of the shouting but the buildings were too tall for us to see anything. "Stay focused!" The lieutenant told us. "Focus on our zone and we will be successful!" The three of us got our weapons ready. Adam was the most eager to fight.

"Are you ready to watch my back?" He asked me. "That fancy new blade of yours can't make up for lack of skill!"

"That's why I'm here to take care of you both," Alice said. Her comment opened the door for more banter between the two. As usual, I just stood aside and listened until the lieutenant told them to shut up. Alice was embarrassed and apologized to him before calling Adam childish. Moments later, a number of large, smoking orbs flew over the wall, crashing into the ground and buildings.

The orbs exploded on impact and a creature would appear through the smoke. We got right to work eliminating them. My sword had started glowing as soon as the sun set and continued to glow brighter as it came in contact with the enemy.

"Wait a minute," Adam said between attacks. "How can they exist in the light?"

"The light does nothing to stronger creatures except keep them from immersing themselves in the shadow and moving around," one of the soldiers said. This was definitely new to us. Now I thought back to the battle before that nearly killed us and how the shadow creatures had to possess people to operate in the light. Does that mean they were the weakest kind? Then does that also mean the Mayor was a only hosting weak creature? Maybe we were in farther over our heads than we thought.

The fighting continued off and on for hours and all sorts of dark monsters came flying over the wall as time went on. Alice's was getting all the money out of her new staff and more. It amplified her spells far beyond what her hands could and allowed for her to cast numerous healing spells without tiring her out nearly as fast. Her magic revitalized all of us throughout our battles and kept us going far longer than we normally would have been able to. Alice's healing spells felt much different than Glinda's. It was like a living thing that was running through my veins and empowering me. Each time she cast a healing spell on someone, the green glow flowed throughout their entire body before migrating specifically to whatever injury they had.

Adam was on fire tonight. He had more kills than anyone else in our zone. At times, he would even hop in and finish off someone else's fight, including some of my own. It became more annoying as the night went on. During one of our short reprieves, I confronted him about it. "I'm just trying to help out; we're a team, right?" He said, patting my shoulder. "That new sword may be nice, but it doesn't hide when you're struggling," he said with a smile before getting a drink of water. I was a little irritated by his words, but I knew how playfully competitive he can get, especially in the heat of battle, so I decided to let it slide. *Fine*, I thought to myself, *I'll just fight even harder and show him up instead.* I knew competition was healthy and convinced myself that it would all okay... when I had the most kills.

The next wave came in the form of attacks on the wall. We first heard hundreds of knocks from the other side that sounded like someone was peppering the wall with arrows. Then a series of dart-like missiles of darkness, much like what we'd seen from the Mayor, pierced through the wall. We all ducked or ran for cover while a few people sustained injuries. Alice reacted immediately to those hit, but the darkness began to spread all over their bodies until it fully consumed them before evaporating into the air. Following the spray of darts were scores of extremely flexible monsters that bled through the holes in the wall. They could wind their bodies and limbs into all different directions to dodge and attack. They had three sharp claws instead of hands and left countless of deep cuts in their victims. Alice did the best she could to heal everyone but there were just too many people, too many injuries, too many monsters, and she even ended up having to protect herself, as well.

At the end of the attack, one person who originally didn't get swallowed by one of the darts, was found dead. Alice was devastated. It was the first time she had lost someone. Adam tried to console her while the lieutenant screamed at everyone, including her. "Can you give us a minute?!" Adam screamed back at him. The two then stepped up to each other, neither of them blinking as they argued. I jumped in between them to calm the situation.

"Listen, we don't have time for this!" I shouted. "They're coming back and we need to be on our guard!"

"Then tell your companion to get her shit together," the lieutenant said. "We need a healer!"

I knelt down beside Alice and calmly told her how valuable she was to us.

"Hey, listen... it sucks. We all know that and we're feeling it, too. It's not solely your fault; it's all of ours. The rest of us should've done a better job keeping an eye on each other," I said as I put an arm around her. "It is your job to heal us, yes, but it is the rest of us, as a team, to keep each other alive. We're responsible for keeping an eye on each other, not just you. You're there to heal us so we can continue watching each other's backs. Therefore, you did nothing wrong. His death is tragic and it's on us. Particularly me, because I'm too stupid to figure out how to use this thing." I was looking at my sword as I finished speaking.

I started off trying to make Alice feel better but as my speech went on I found myself mainly saying whatever came to my mind. As the words came out, though, I began to feel them more and more. The last line was complete truth because I really did feel that way. Ever since this weapon had come to me, I'd done very little to understand it. Everyone else was progressing at a quick pace while I moved like a slug to master my abilities. I'm the one getting left behind and it just cost someone's life. Now I was really starting to get myself down. I snapped out of it when we were hit with another attack much like the last.

Alice pulled herself together when the fighting started. I think some of the other soldiers overheard my speech to her because this assault went much smoother than the last. Maybe it was me, or maybe we just knew what to expect from these creatures, I don't know, but either way, we were more successful this time around. We had to endure one more attack from those creatures before we got to experience a prolonged break.

Barely ten minutes later, we endured another barrage of flying orbs. Before we could finish them, the wall was darted again and two more soldiers, comrades, husbands... fathers... were swallowed by shadows. We didn't have enough time to mourn the dead or even move their bodies before the same rain of missiles fell from the sky. Someone from the top of a building called them out and we ran for cover. I was nearly through a doorway when I tripped and twisted my ankle. I shouted and pain and rolled to look at the injury but I couldn't find my ankle under a moving, black shadow. I had been hit. I could feel it creeping along my skin and each inch hurt worse than the last. It felt like my bones were on fire. I shouted for Alice but she was around the corner and all I saw was a flash of green bathe another soldier. I shouted again for someone else but nobody was immediately nearby. I didn't know what to do so I rubbed the blackness down my leg to try and push it away. I was sweating furiously and couldn't catch my breath. The burning was growing more intense. Once I touched it, it began spreading over my hands and up my arms. It felt like teeth biting my fingers off one joint at a time. I screamed again in pain and fell backwards. As I fell I threw my arms down to grab ahold of something, anything, just to hold onto. I wanted to grab some kind of support to squeeze or even find water to stop the burning. Anything at all. My left hand eventually touched my sword that I had dropped earlier. I grabbed it and squeezed as hard as I could, still screaming from the pain. Behind my closed eyes I saw a bright light to my left. I looked to see my sword brimming with light. It shone brighter and brighter and the blackness began to fade away across my hand and up my arm. I gave the sword to my right hand where it did the same thing and then smacked the sword at my legs. The light from my sword destroyed the darkness, not even allowing it to fade away into the air like it had done after swallowing my companions before. I stood up, sore and pissed off, and ready to fight again.

The rain of darts came once again and another person got hit. This time, I didn't even run for cover. I swung my sword at the air and the afterimage of light that came from it destroyed at least half-a-dozen missiles. I ran to the soldier who was hit and stabbed the wound with the tip of my sword causing it to eliminate the expanding threat. I was hungry for more now–angry and ready for more darkness to challenge me... but no more came. That was the end of the siege.

Hours later we were ordered to bed down at our inn. No more enemies appeared by that time. The captain of the night watch was dumbfounded. "This wasn't any worse than a typical night," he said. "I'm not sure whether or not this is a good sign, but for now, we'll stick to the plan. Get some rest."

The walk back was awful. I was so happy to finally realize more of my sword's capabilities and, sure enough, it had been too late. *What good am I if I can't help anyone on time?* I had saved one person, yes, but had watched four people get swallowed up. *I need to stop letting the situation get out of hand before my emotions kick in again so I can start helping people instead.* Everyone else was busy discussing their experiences but I remained quiet. Glinda approached me and asked why I was so quiet. I told her I was just tired, which wasn't a lie; I really was tired. I was tired of not being able to act like the team leader I should be and tired of being too weak.

Back at the inn, breakfast as already cooked and waiting for at a table. Our guide had been so kind as to request for us a meal with no fish. We were treated with a meal much like back home with a few other unknown delicacies. The food made me feel better but all I really wanted to do was go to sleep. I was upset with myself and my body was getting tired. I just needed to sleep and be left alone to deal with myself. I knew that if I could just fall asleep, I could sleep away a lot of these emotions and hopefully feel better when I woke up.

Chapter 11

The horses we were given were some of the best quality I had seen which made them rather unusual for a place like this. The stable master told us they were his best horses and were mainly used for hauling lumber across the vast expanse of fields surrounding the lake so we could rely on them more than any other horses we may be accustomed to.

A lieutenant was at the stable to give us maps and general directions of possible enemy locations. The surrounding mountains had all been explored in the past and that knowledge allowed them to have a some sort of ideas for the best places a military leader would stage a command post as well as possible attack points. The hills and mountain ranges weren't too particularly tall but compared to how low the river in the valley was they seemed much higher. Both ranges were as wide as they were tall with only a gradual grade so it was easy for the horses to make the ascent.

For the first day, we were given a section of the northern mountain range and three days in total to cover the entire range before returning to the city. If we were unsuccessful in locating the head of the snake, so to speak, we would be tasked to cover the southern range. I really hoped this would be it because the map showed the southern range as being much larger and leading farther south into much higher mountains.

As we closed in on the first section of mountain, I began to wonder how thorough this plan really was. Anyone atop any part of these ranges would be able to see our every move. If there was a cave system or means of retreat, they would have more than enough time to escape to it. We all discussed that possibility as well as others since there was only so much to talk about on our hours-long trek.

Obviously, we had no luck at all by the time we reached the peak. The sun was falling over the horizon by the time we made it and then I began to wonder why on earth we had to leave when we did; our whole first day was wasted just getting to one place.

Then came the worst part: nighttime. We were overlooking the city and had no choice but to watch the upcoming events unfold. I'm not sure if the captain got the days wrong in his weariness or if things were just changing but from where we were it looked like tonight was one of the big sieges. We got to watch the torches being lit across the whole lake and it looked even more gorgeous from here. Like a million fireflies resting on the water.

It wasn't too long into the siege when we began to see torches go out. The creatures were attacking the lights to create a shield for their weaker troops. I assumed there was an abundance of the grunts because, in my mind, it would only make sense for some stronger creatures to come in first and open a path for a multitude of weaklings to flood in and overrun the defending soldiers. Unfortunately, that seemed to be the case because lights in the city weren't going out in random places but in waves from edges of the town. At times, we would see torches flare back up in the occupied areas only to go out again. Beelines of lights moved quickly from certain areas of town, like the city center and guard towers, to reoccupy taken sections. Sometimes we would see those lines get extinguished. One actually turned into a burning building. Other buildings caught on fire, as well. Luckily the city was on a lake so there wouldn't be much spread.

We considered ourselves at least slightly fortunate for not being close enough to hear the screams, but I think they still rang through my ears. It could've just been my imagination but I thought I could hear the agony in the air. I could only imagine what sort of chaos was going on in the dark areas of town. Families, women, children, babies, even pets were being consumed in whatever gruesome way the shadows chose. Maybe they were being possessed and used against their men who were fighting? What kind of psychological attacks were taking place on the bridges below us?

Glinda was especially hurt by this. Tears were running down her cheeks but she still wouldn't take her eyes off it. "That's it," she said as she stood up. Pulling out her wand and twirling it out in front of her, countless pixies were released. "Why didn't I think of this sooner?" she asked herself through the tears. An unimaginable number of pixies flew like a swarm of locusts down to the village. When they reached their destination, they broke into waves and flooded every dark sector of the lake. As the pixies pushed away the darkness, we were able to see more orange firelights pop up all across town. Glinda then fell down to a sitting position, a little out of breath. She wore herself out by dumping so much magic into that move, but her efforts had saved the entire city.

In a matter of minutes, the city of Ruciam went from being about fifty-percent covered by shadow to a shimmering pool of sunlight. Glinda then made another impressive maneuver. A few minutes after all the darkness had been pushed from the city, the swarm of pixies circled outside the walls until they made a large ring that spun for nearly ten minutes. Then, half of them made their way back to us while the rest stayed behind to conduct, what I assumed to be, healing spells for the townspeople and soldiers. The pixies that returned to Glinda crowded around her and faded out with flashes of light. She took a deep breath as it happened and then smiled. "Much better," she said.

"What was that just now?" I asked.

"I had them turn back into magic power for me," she said like it was nothing unusual. But that was new. And cool. Before, the pixies would just flash out of existence and that was it. Now, I guess, she could regenerate her own power when she was done with them.

Twenty-two hours later we set up camp at the highest peak of the northern mountain range. It was farther west than the city and overlooked a landscape that went on forever. The Egura river wound around hills as far west as the eye could see. The expanse of fields was populated by very little forest. "Wow," Alice and Eric both said at the same time. "Wow indeed," I responded, watching the sun set at the same place the river fell off on the horizon.

I turned to lay out my bed furs and saw Glinda release another mass of pixies to aid the city.

"This is stupid," Adam said as he laid down. "We've busted our asses to cover this entire mountain range only to find nothing. Nothing at all!"

"Oh, shut up," Dorothy said.

"Doesn't it bother you?" he asked her. "At the very least, it should seem fishy." He made a good point. The direction of some of the assaults have come from this area. Even if enemies that had been stationed here saw us yesterday, there is no way they could have moved across the valley and to the southern range quickly enough without us spotting even a little bit of movement. We had stayed as high up in the mountains as possible all day and didn't see a single thing. Glinda even had more than thirty pixies patrolling around us and not a single clue has been found.

"You don't think…" Adam started, before biting his tongue.

"What? Conspiracy?" Alice asked him.

"Exactly," he replied.

Whoa. I hadn't thought of that one, but it made a little bit of sense. More sense than we had come across lately, at least. We decided to focus on that topic.

"We were given three days, but perhaps we should head back tomorrow morning and see what we can dig up," Glinda suggested. "This all just seems too unusual." She was right. We were making, literally, zero progress on this mission.

"I think it might be appropriate to make an appointment with the mayor for tomorrow afternoon," Eric said.

We giddied-up the ponies as much as they would allow and arrived back to the stable master early in the afternoon then headed directly for the town hall. The mayor was in some kind of meeting so we had to wait nearly an hour in the lobby. When he finally called us into his conference hall, the smell of cooked fish greeted our nostrils. It wasn't until I saw the stains of food at the corners of his mouth that I realized why.

"You're quite early," he said to us sternly. "Have you met with success?"

"We think so," I began. "Sir, we believe the threat may be coming from inside." He was bewildered at first and then angry.

"How dare you suggest such a thing? My city council far outclasses those of other cities and my officers are of the highest quality. My men have sweeped this city every single day and not once have they found anything even remotely matching your suspicion." We made an attempt to explain ourselves but he wouldn't have any of it and quickly dismissed us. On our way out Adam said, "do you think…"

"…he's hiding something," Dorothy finished.

After leaving the building we went straight for the guard tower we were at the other night to meet with the tired captain of the night watch. The lieutenant that I worked with the other night met us in the command room instead and was dressed differently than I remembered.

"It's good to see you're all still alive," he said to us. "What news do you have from your recent mission?"

"We need to see the captain," Adam said loudly, nearly startling the man.

He took a slow breath and then said, "you're looking at him." We were confused and he could tell so he went on, "our recent commander met with an unfortunate accident in the line of duty during the big assault a couple nights ago." We asked him more about it and he explained to us that the untimely death perplexed him since the captain was always accompanied by soldiers and the death occurred after the pixies began clearing much of the city. "The pixies you sent us eliminated ninety-percent of the enemy force but one of the brutes managed to penetrate the captain's defenses and attack him with poison. They must be getting stronger or smarter because we haven't encountered poison before." We offered him our condolences and left to gather our thoughts.

"Poison…" Dorothy said as we left the tower. "Hey, look," Adam said pointing to the end of the street. A man in a long, black coat and wide-brimmed, black hat was turning the corner quickly as we exited the building.

"That's the guy you noticed earlier, isn't it, Eric?" I asked, remembering he briefly mentioned the man to me on our first day in Ruciam.

"Indeed," Eric replied. "I caught a glimpse of him behind us on our way here after we left the town hall."

"Why don't you two go back up the tower and ask for a private audience with the new captain," I suggested as I scanned our surroundings.

"Oh! Can I go, too?" Alice asked raising her hand.

"No," Adam said. "You'll just scare him off." Alice then chased him into the front door of the tower and Eric followed.

The two girls and I found a bench nearby and sat in a way that we could see all around us. We threw around ideas about what might be going on but there were just too many mysteries to suggest any one answer. The others finally returned about fifteen minutes later with the new captain and his lieutenant.

"Follow me," he said.

He didn't say another word as he led us down a series of alleyways. The lieutenant brought up the rear, turning often to watch behind us. Finally, we came to a dead end and a broken, wooden door. The captain brought us inside and requested a torch to be lit by Dorothy. The room wasn't empty but hadn't been occupied in quite some time. Broken furniture had been pushed against the walls to reveal a barren floor and a small, wooden trapdoor. The captain opened it up and had us descend the metal steps.

We found ourselves in the sewers underneath the city and the captain took the lead again. "How and why is there a sewer system underneath a huge lake?" Dorothy asked. "Well, the lake itself isn't really a lake," the captain informed us. "It's just a man-made system of canals in the middle of a river and isn't very deep at all. At one time, when there weren't any sewers, everyone just tossed their waste into the river. Not long after, towns downstream began to complain. After that, Ruciam's mayor at the time set up a committee to figure out a way to preserve the river by copying the sewer system at the capital. This is ironic because the very same mayor later instigated a massive 'lumber acquisition initiative' to expand the city and create farmland." By the time he was finished speaking we were in front of another wooden door that seemed to be much newer. He had to unlock it with a key. There was light coming from inside.

Chapter 12

Six large men sat around a horseshoe-like table while a fire burned in the center. Torches lined the walls that held bookcases, cabinets, chests, weapon racks, and other things that might be found in a house or barracks. My first thought after being surprised was how there was no smoke filling the room but then I noticed an opening in the ceiling about the fire pit that I assumed, if they were being secretive, led up a chimney.

"Have a seat," the captain said as the men all greeted us. There was plenty of room; fourteen chairs in total were positioned around the table and there was still elbow room. The captain remained standing and introduced each person sitting. They were all former soldiers, two being former officers and four being assistants to officers. Now, they worked covert operations for select members of the military. "You might wonder why there would be a need for covert operations," the captain said to us. "And you will continue to wonder. I'm not sure what your small town was like but even before the darkness came the world has always been a nasty place, just in different ways throughout the years."

We were told to tell everything we know to the men at the table so we did. Each of us gave our input while all of them sat quietly, evaluating every tiny bit of information that came from our mouths. After we finished, the only sound that could be heard was the crackling fire. Everyone was staring at it, pondering the stories that had just been told. Eventually, one of the men slammed his hand on the table and said, "I knew it! I've been saying all these years that man was corrupt! Haven't I?"

"Relax," said another one. "There's still not enough information to determine the mayor is the root cause. He could be controlled or manipulated."

"Yeah, with food."

They then got into bad-mouthing the mayor and making colorful comments about his weight, the absence of women in his chambers, how he can't see certain parts of his body when he looks down, and the shortage of seafood they've noticed since he was elected into office.

"Elected," the first man said making quotation marks in the air with his fingers. "We all know he ate his predecessor." I laughed a little because I thought it was another joke but apparently there was a conspiracy theory that the previous mayor actually had been cooked alive and eaten by the current mayor on the day of his inauguration.

After quite a while of discussing the ridiculousness of the mayor, the captain shouted above everyone to get our discussion back on the right track.

"What can we do about this?"

"Night infiltration," someone said.

"Espionage," came another comment.

"Assassination... publicly."

"Alright, alright," the captain said. "They all sound like great ideas but we need to settle on a plan for A, B, and C and then figure out how. But, for now, I've got to get back above ground and prepare for this evening's entertainment."

"What do you want us to do?" I asked. "Same positions as before?"

"No, your team needs to leave town immediately. Begin your next mission in the southern mountains. It'll seem suspicious if you stick around."

"But how will we help you solve these mysteries if we're away for five days?" Alice asked. She just wanted to stay near the captain.

"You can't be directly involved," he replied. "You all are too obvious. If you just do what you were brought here to do, that'll be enough. Otherwise, all eyes would be on your every move in this city. You've already done more than enough for us."

We didn't make it very far away from the city before the sun set. The shouting started by the time we made it to the base of the first mountain. Glinda had already deployed pixies so we didn't worry too much even though we heard a lot more shouting than we thought we should with so many lights floating about.

We kept going late into the night. None of us were really ready to sleep; our minds were too busy replaying the day's events. Personally, I was glad we weren't alone anymore. It was comforting to know we were working with such capable warriors. The others felt the same way and, as time went on, we even created backstories for each person.

The mountain we were climbing was connected to a range much like the last one except it continued on farther south, getting higher and connecting to another range. Our mission was to inspect this range that ran along the river valley and some of the higher mountains behind it. Two days for this range and two days for the mountains behind it and one day to return. We were so set on our conspiracy theories, however, that we collaborated and decided to make this trip less than four days. None of us felt the need to be out here any longer than necessary if the real threat was back in the city.

Once we reached the summit it was the middle of the night and the lights were still burning in the city. We had five hours until sunrise and decided that was all we were going to take to sleep. Glinda set up some pixies around us and we all tried to relax.

The next day was another dull one. Up and down hills over and over again. Nonstop. All. Day. These mountains were more barren than the last ones. The other range provided quite a number of trees to shade us but there were almost none in sight down here. Every so often we would find small pools of water that had been collected by what little bit of rain had fallen. It was obvious that not much precipitation regularly accumulated down here, probably thanks to the larger mountains directly south.

Glinda once again sent pixies to the city later that evening and then fell right to sleep. I think summoning so many each day was wearing on her. The rest of us went ahead and decided to get a full eight hours of sleep tonight and the next morning we tried to talk her into not sending so many this time. "No, because we have no idea when the next big assault will be and I refuse to let people suffer now that I know I can help." She was a lot like Eric in a protectionist sort of way. The two of them seriously believed that if someone had the power to help another person, they were required to. Her desire to help others was far beyond anyone else I had met. She wouldn't budge on the matter so we didn't try to push the subject again.

We circled around the highest mountain the next day and decided to not even go to the summit. On one hand, we could see everything and get a good look around, but we really wanted to get back to the city and help with the secret mission. "What do you say we head back tomorrow morning?" I asked the group. "We'll descend the other end of the range and come back into the city from the northeastern gate." Everyone agreed to that; we were all on the same page and I thought that was a good thing right now.

Heading in towards the evening, we started noticing peculiar things from the corners of our eyes. For over an hour, every so often, one of us would catch a glimpse of movement from our peripherals.

Eventually, Glinda just started sending pixies out in whatever direction one of us would call out. However, the fourth pixie she released didn't even come back. We had just kept on moving when she sent it out but after a while she turned back to recall it. It never came. "Hey, I may have something," she told us. We all followed her in the direction she had sent it. On the other side of a small cliff were some bushes where she had noticed movement. As we approached, a poof of black smoke appeared and shot to our left and down a hill to the south. Dorothy fired three fireballs at it but they missed as it flew inches above the ground, darting around rocks and other obstacles. We kicked our horses into high gear to pursue it.

The sun was setting and we still hadn't caught up with it. It was leading us on a wild goose chase and every pixie that Glinda sent after it was just attacked. The thing took us around a higher peak where we found some plants that Dorothy set on fire to block its path. It tried to dart another way but Alice caused a vine to come up from the ground and grab it. Since the target seemed to only be made of smoke, she infused the vine with magical energy so it could hold onto the enemy–another new trait she had picked up.

When we moved in close it just… popped. Poof, it vanished. "What the heck?" Adam said.

"Anybody pay attention to where we'd been going?" Alice asked.

"I did for about a mile then one of the turns got me confused. I think we're just directly south of the city, though," Eric replied. He was good; I wasn't even sure how many miles we had gone. We chased that stupid thing for a while and it was now dark.

"Oh no!" Glinda shouted. "I didn't send out the pixies!" She turned around and created more than she had ever done before. Hundreds of sparkling diamonds jetted north towards town. She told us that when half of them returned this time she would keep one to lead us back.

I was the first one to wake up the next morning. The air was already warming up from the sun which was high enough in the sky that I guessed it to be well past eight in the morning. I took a drink of water, stood up, stretched, and then stopped. My brain finally clicked on and I realized we were sleeping in much later than usual. I looked around at everyone else snoozing but couldn't find any of the pixies that Glinda stationed around us nor were there any pixies that she had sent to the city. I woke everyone up so they could weigh in on this.

Glinda was the most confused. She couldn't sense any of her little minions. Dorothy inspected the area around us and couldn't find any traces of magic activity.

"None at all?" Alice asked her.

"None. Not even our own. Glinda and I set up lights around us last night, as usual, and there isn't even a trace of that." We skipped breakfast to get back to the city as quickly as our horses would let us.

We made it to the edge of the mountains about an hour later to find the city still intact. Nothing seemed out of the ordinary but we were so far away that it was hard to tell. Glinda sent a handful of pixies to go on ahead and check things out while we high-tailed it down to the valley.

The pixies returned when we made it to the base of the ridge and Glinda translated their little dances for us.

"They say we don't need to hurry and that nothing seems unusual."

"Do we trust their judgement, though?" Dorothy asked suspiciously. Glinda shot her a dirty look, one that we don't see very often.

"Of course!" From there we took a little more time but still kept a brisk pace.

Sure enough, the city seemed fine. Everyone was milling about their usual duties; mingling and shopping as if everything was normal. Boats were even still arriving and leaving as normally as every other day.

"Seems normal enough," Adam said as we made our way towards the stables.

"Yeah.. but that doesn't explain the missing pixies," I noted. Even the stable master was acting normal and greeted us heartily.

We decided to visit the captain at the guard tower before reporting into the city hall. All of the guards inside seemed more relaxed than usual but nothing weird was going on. When we got to the captain's office, one of his lieutenants informed us that he hadn't been in yet today and was probably off doing the typical rounds of inspection that fall within a leader's duties. Instead of just brushing this off and waiting for him, we figured we should pay a visit to that secret room from before and see what we can dig up.

We left the tower and took the alleyway that we were led down the other day. After about ten minutes of walking and two turns, we realized that not a single one of us remembered exactly how to get there.

"All of the buildings look the same from down here!" Alice complained.

"It's alright!" Adam shouted. "I remember this bridge over here so we're on the right track!" He took the lead and we followed him around three more turns before we found ourselves at a dead end. Unfortunately, this particular dead end had no broken door, or any door for that matter.

"Okay, he's out of the group," Alice said.

We wandered around for at least another hour before people started complaining about food. We had skipped breakfast and barely ate any lunch and once someone mentioned it I began to feel the same way. I decided to give things a few more minutes and then we could get some food from a restaurant while we figure out our next move. After walking around another block, we passed an alleyway that led to a dead end and a broken, wooden door.

"Let's hope the same thing that happened up there doesn't happen down here," I said with a slight chuckle as we traversed the sewers. "Oh my gosh don't say that!" Glinda whined. I knew we'd be okay, though, because we didn't make any real turns before. We passed three paths along the righthand wall and each led to a metal gate so we knew those weren't it. The fourth one held the wooden door we hoped was what we were looking for.

To our dismay, the room was empty. There wasn't even a fire burning to indicate that someone had just been there or would be returning. "Search the room," I said. "Maybe there's a clue or something about their plan or where someone may be." We separated to scan the room and then heard a voice behind us.

There is no one else here. We turned to find an empty doorway.

Right here, the voice said again as a purple and black flame lit up on the embers of the fire pit. "What have you done with them?" Adam shouted over the roaring flames while drawing both swords. *Let me show you,* the voice said sounding almost as if it came from a smiling face this time. The fire flared up, growing enormously hot, and exploded across us and the rest of the room only seconds later causing furniture to scatter and the door to blow off its hinges.

My ears were ringing and my head was pounding. I was certain I had to be dead. That was the largest explosion I've ever witnessed but, besides my new headache, I didn't feel any other pain. I opened my eyes and dropped my hands to see that I was fine. My shiny sword was in my right hand and I wondered if it protected me when I brought it up to my face out of reflex. When I looked around, I noticed everyone else was okay, as well. Could it be possible that, out of fear, my sword, or myself, had done something to protect all of us?

"Nice work, Glinda," Dorothy commented as she walked around the fire pit.

"Thanks," Glinda replied. "I was afraid my barriers wouldn't hold up, but I had a little bit of time."

"You saved us?" I asked.

"Duh," Alice said. "Didn't you notice? She began raising barriers in front of us when that creepy voice first echoed from that fire!"

"Huh… well, thank you," I said. The rest of the team thanked her too and praised her quick reaction.

Glinda just flipped her hair and said, "oh, don't flatter me, boys."

The explosion destroyed everything in the room besides us and left no trace of magic. Now we knew something was going on from inside the city and Dorothy wondered if it had something to do with what we experienced in the mountains.

"What if…" she began. "What if this enemy created that smokeball as a diversion to lead us farther away? Then, while we were asleep, it snuffed out our magic and put a spell on us?"

"It must've really wanted us to stay away," I wondered. "But why? Are we that much of a threat? Or is there another reason?" As each day passed since coming to this city, we found more and more questions to ask than were being answered. Maybe it was finally time to return to the town hall.

Chapter 13

Everything was business as usual and nothing out of the ordinary happened during our visit which meant we were nearly thrown out. One of the mayor's servants followed us out of the hall and presented us with a bag of gold coins, a message to us, and another letter than he said needs to be delivered downstream to the city of Linareus.

"Awesome," Adam said. "Another freaking delivery. Is that all we're good for these days?"

"Yeah, it's getting kind of repetitive," I acknowledged.

"What do you say we stick around for one more night and see what happens?" Alice asked.

"No good," I told her as I scanned the letter to us. "It says here that we have a boat waiting for us from the southwestern dock in a few hours."

"If his job is to take us downstream then he'll still be there tomorrow at noon," Dorothy said walking off. We followed along, mulling over her last statement. She led us to the foreign restaurant that we always went to so we sat down to eat and discuss our next course of action.

After we ate, I pulled out the bag of gold and dumped it on the table. "Whoa!" Adam exclaimed. Actually, we all expressed our excitement. This was the most gold we've ever had at one time.

"Hold on a minute," Dorothy commented as we were counting it all. "Am I the only person who isn't forgetting our suspicions? Doesn't it seem like they're trying to get us out of here awfully quickly?" She was right. Nobody seemed to care that we came back early from both of our missions and yet we still got paid an enormous amount of money while a boat is already waiting to take us to a city that is over a week away by foot?

"Maybe we should stay for one night," I said as we put the money back into the bag.

Back at the inn, we found our rooms cleared. The innkeeper informed us that we had been checked out and our rooms rented to someone else. The rest of the rooms were also booked, as well, including those at two other inns.

"I get that this is a busy town, but how often are all the inns occupied when there isn't even so much as a festival going on?" Alice questioned.

"I guess they really are trying to get rid of us," I said.

"That's fine," Dorothy said. "We'll just camp outside the gate along with all the other squatters." She kind of intimidated me when she got like this. Whenever she didn't get her way she would throw away any respect for authority and start finding ways to get what she wants. At least this time none of us were getting hurt or in serious trouble... yet.

We didn't even get our bed furs rolled out all the way before a soldier walked through the campsite shouting for us. Glinda started to call out to him but Dorothy slapped a hand over her mouth. The guard must've heard something because he came straight over with an angry look on his face.

"What are you kids doing? Do you have any idea how long you've kept your boat captain waiting?"

"We didn't feel prepared to leave just yet so we decided to stay one more night and leave in the morning," I told him.

"And you didn't think to tell him that?" The soldier asked. "He has a schedule to keep to and more business to handle after dropping you off. You may have just cost him fifty-percent or more of his next payment for being late!" Upon hearing that, it was apparent that we really were no longer wanted in this city and there was no way we could argue so we packed up and gloomily made our way to the opposite dock.

The boat captain was furious. Instead of casually traveling along with the current, he now had to let down the sails and we were going to have to help his crew row into the night to make up for lost time. If we caused him to be late on his next appointment he said we would have to make up for any money he lost so he could feed his family. I honestly felt pretty bad for making him late. Dorothy, on the other hand, didn't. She was more irritated at the way we had been kicked out of the city. I guess I was a little irritated, too. More than anything, though, I was worried. We all knew something bad was going on here and there was nothing we could do about it. We weren't just leaving behind an active threat that we were very much aware of, but we were also leaving behind acquaintances that we had made who had disappeared after we informed them of the bizarre happenings in the city. We didn't know if they were alive or dead or if we had something to do with their disappearance. I could see it in everyone else's faces, too. We all felt defeated. We had a sack of gold and a new mission and yet we were still failures.

I didn't even want to get up the next morning. It wasn't because my arms were sore from rowing for six hours. It wasn't because my bed was comfortable like feathers, because it wasn't. It wasn't even a bed. There were two 'bedrooms' below deck and each of them held nine hammocks. My back was sore from sleeping in the same position all night and I felt a little seasick from swaying so much with my eyes closed. Even opening my eyes didn't help because my face was so close to the ceiling and the wall that it caused me to freak out a little bit.

No, the reason why I didn't want to get up was because the defeat was still weighing on me. We had lost people in the past, but we always completed our mission and at least sort of saved the day. The deaths hadn't been in vain because we had always been successful. Now we were being forced to run away from the enemy and leave innocent people to an unholy doom. Once again, I was letting someone down. Lives would be lost and families would be broken while I had the power to do something about it and I just left. I just left without putting up a fight, without even taking a chance to make things right.

I'm pathetic, I thought to myself. Why can't I be more like Dorothy? *She's a better leader and hero than I ever could be.*

Later on, I found Eric on the deck, sitting and staring at the waves. He didn't feel like talking and I think I knew why. This situation was eating away at him more than me because something inside him drove him to care about other people's safety and well-being far beyond his own. While normal people naturally feel compelled to help others, Eric was more like a mother looking out for her newborn child. It didn't matter if it was people or animals, anything that was in danger was his newborn child. Now, he was being forced to leave behind thousands of newborn children while vultures circled overhead and wolves watched from the shadows. After sitting with him for a while, I began to think of Glinda. I had to check on her because I was certain she was feeling rotten inside at least as much as Eric. I got up, patted him on the shoulder, and went to search for our team's little angel.

I wandered towards the back of the boat and eventually heard the sounds of different spells so I followed to find the source. The boat had two levels of decks in the rear and all three girls were on the top floor. I had expected to see Glinda in a dismal mood but she seemed quite fine. Better than fine, in fact. Her and Alice were casting different spells at each other as if they were playfully fighting but the looks on both their faces were serious. Dorothy was sitting at a small table watching them with her chin propped on her hands. I sat down next to her and asked what was going on.

"The two of them were feeling pretty heartbroken about leaving the city the way we did so they're blowing off some steam as per my suggestion," she told me in a dull tone.

"And how are you feeling?" I asked. She didn't say anything for a moment and then said she was doing just fine in the same bland voice. I didn't want to press anymore because we had all learned before not to question her when she's in a bad mood. I wasn't sure, but I would venture to guess she was in one of those moods right now. Even as tough as she always is, it was apparent that the situation was bugging her, too. I sat a little longer just to watch the girls dance back and forth with flashes of light illuminating the entire deck. It really was an elegant display of power.

I decided to find Adam and see how he was doing. I think it helped me to talk to people when I get down like this. Typically, I didn't want to, but I tried to convince myself it was for the best. Not just for me, but maybe for them. I enjoyed having regular chats with Adam, though. He was my best friend and we thought pretty much exactly alike so our conversations could go from serious to hilarious in seconds. I searched almost the entire vessel before one of the sailors directed me to the front. He was standing and leaning against two ropes that attached to one of the masts.

"Nice view, huh?" I asked as I walked up and leaned on the balustrade that lined the deck. We were passing through a thick forested region and mountains rose in the distance.

"Kind of reminds me of back home," he said. I looked around some more and found him to be right. We'd seen all this before during some of our adventures in the woods outside home. "What are we even doing?" He asked me after a long silence. I asked him what he meant by that.

"What's our purpose right now? Just to deliver letters and run errands? All we've really done is go from place to place on someone else's agenda and we've gotten nowhere close to stopping this threat."

"What are you getting at? That everything we've done so far has been for nothing?" I asked, a little irritated.

"I'm not say that, but I'm wondering if we haven't been doing things exactly right. Maybe we can do things a little differently. We can still get some work done for people, but we can also have our own mission."

"Our 'mission' is to stop this darkness for good," I said a little angrier now that he would be questioning it as if it wasn't so obvious.

"And how has that gone for us so far? Everytime we leave a place the enemy will just return. We're just floating along to wherever someone else wants us to go and doing whatever they want us to do, no better than this damn boat! The path we're traveling has left a whole city at the mercy of the enemy already! What if that happens again?"

"It won't because we're going to stop it anyway we can!"

"But how?? We have no plan! We need a new agenda; one of our own!"

"Then what do you suggest? What kind of master plan have you been working on?" He didn't say anything for a few moments. He went to the opposite railing and leaned against it.

"Maybe we need to start asking questions... Instead of just going wherever someone points, maybe we should ask for directions of our own. With any luck, we could locate a source of some kind."

I gave his suggestion a little thought. He was right. So far we've just been doing work for different mayors, work that could be done by six of their own soldiers. I liked to think of our team as something special who should have a higher purpose than what we've been doing so far. "And besides," he started again. "You have that fancy new sword that is designed for killing these things. You're something extra special." He said that in an almost sarcastic tone but I brushed it off as a playful insult like usual.

The bell rang for lunch so we headed back to the kitchen to grab some food. The captain made an announcement during the meal that, thanks to generous winds, we were making great time and should arrive on schedule as long as nothing bad happens. I hated that he added that at the end because, for us, that almost always meant there was a change coming. I looked up at the sky after the announcement just to see if any dark clouds were approaching.

The rest of the day went fairly smoothly. We still had a lot of time before we arrived so we volunteered to work around the boat to keep ourselves busy. The captain just laughed at us and said that we didn't have to volunteer because he was going to put us to work tomorrow anyway. I gathered the group together to the back of the boat where the tables were so we could discuss what Adam and I talked about earlier.

"In that case, what should our next move be whenever we arrive?" Dorothy asked, pretty interested in the idea.

"Well, we still have to deliver this letter," I said. "And we can be sure the mayor will have some sort of assignment for us. If you guys haven't noticed yet, the farther west that we travel, the larger the threats seem to be."

"So you're saying that the source could be from somewhere out west?" Alice wondered.

"I'm not sure just yet, but maybe we can ask around about any kind of suspicious activity happening out that way. We lost that opportunity in the last two big cities but Linareus is close to the capital so hopefully we'll run into at least a few interesting characters." Eric then chimed in with his own suggestion, the first time I'd heard him speak today, "we should keep our eyes and ears open for more corruption. Like in Ruciam, we should be aware that the enemy can take over powerful people and that, for all we know, the capital could be at risk." That was a scary thought. Could it be possible that our own government was already threatened? If the king was being controlled then that could spell doom for the entire country and neighboring countries, as well.

The rest of our voyage was a mix of boring and busy. Us guys were tasked with cleaning topside and helping crew the ship while the girls cleaned and cooked below deck. Whenever we weren't working we would relax together or get in a little bit of exercise. Dorothy and Alice used their magic to help me experiment with my sword so we could all understand it a little better. The light magic from my blade seemed to be more closely related to Glinda's spells, though, so she stepped in, too.

We eventually got bored enough that the three of us guys decided to have wrestling matches. The girls found us on one of the back decks having a three-way battle royale. "Boys are dumb," Alice said to the agreement of the others. I guess the crew shared our discomfort because some of the men joined us and we ended up having a small tournament.

"Boys are dumb," Alice said again.

"We might as well get some milage out of it, though," Dorothy said and started taking bets. Eric proved the most formidable against the grown sailors but in the end we came out without winning anything. It was a great way to pass the time. Afterwards the participating crew members brought us below deck to enjoy some of the barreled ale they had stored in the kitchen. None of us had ever actually been drunk before and the sailors were professionals at it so it made for an interesting night. The girls each had one pint while the rest of us lost count and we ended up puking overboard later that evening.

I woke up on the floor of my room before sunrise. My shirt was missing and I couldn't figure out if I had to pee or throw up again. In all seriousness, I didn't want to move. I had the most splitting headache that I honestly thought I was going to die. The swaying of the boat made me feel even more sick so I ran to the deck and vomited some more. I found a couple sailors up there sprawled out by the edge of the boat and I assumed they had already gone through what was happening to me.

Thirty-six hours later, we finally made port just in time for an early dinner. Thanks to our little wrestling tournament and, apparently we were so much fun to drink with (Adam is the craziest kid they've ever met for some reason), the crew decided to take us to their favorite restaurant in the city. However, the captain reminded them that they are extremely pressed for time and barely had the chance to restock before they had to leave so the guy who won the tournament gave us his winnings and meal recommendations.

  The city was actually really normal, but in a lovely way. It was in valley much like Ruciam but the forest was still sprawling. All of the buildings were made from the same kind of tan-colored stone and most resembled each other. Box shapes repeated themselves on every city block. It was also hard to figure out the size of the city because of all the vegetation. Plants grew on balconies and vines ran along walls while trees grew alongside the roads. "Are there any other colors here besides tan and green?" Dorothy said almost disgustingly. We all turned to look at her. "What?" she asked. We just stared at her for a moment and kept going, trying not to laugh. Out of our entire group, she was the only one of us that stuck with one specific color: black. Then again, it kind of suited her. Her personality wouldn't match Glinda's bright colors or even Alice's nature colors. "I love it," Alice said as she used her magic to make some plants dance. Dorothy walked past her and the plants ignited in small flames.

We found the restaurant near what we thought was the city center. It was a large open circle with an enormous fountain in the middle. Shops and restaurants lined the outer edge and a quaint church poked out above all the two-story buildings. Our server at the restaurant was one of the nicest old ladies I've ever met and noticed we were foreigners right away so she was happy to answer any question we had.

We decided to keep things pretty normal in the beginning by asking about the city, the community, neighboring villages, and other general questions any interested newcomer may have. We learned the history of the city and how it became heavily focused on environmental preservation. "This city is actually the home of the leading center for environmental research in the country," she told us. "They do guided tours two times a day because many students, teachers, and researchers visit here all year 'round."

Due to its location at the intersection of major rivers, within a thick forest, and so near the capital, the city is home to a very diverse population of plants, animals, and people. We also found out that the city is relatively small for how popular it is. "Due to the meetin' of two rivers here, the city is split into three districts. Each one has a kind of city center much like this one. We are currently here in the East District," she said, pointing to a spot on a tourism map.

Alice was the most excited about this city. "We HAVE to go visit the research center!" She said to us. "We can check it out after we deliver this message," I assured her. I actually wanted to visit it, as well. There was so much of this world that we didn't know about and I was very eager to learn. Growing up in such a small, isolated town, we didn't really get subjected to everything that was beyond our borders. Even in school we hardly learned about the history, geography, and demographics of our own country. We basically just got taught general things to function in our own society. It wasn't as if anyone was hiding anything from us, there just wasn't a real need for spending so much time learning about a world that we would probably never experience. Since there was nothing significant or special about our town, I wasn't surprised to find that our village wasn't even listed on a single map we had seen so far.

We didn't get to ask too many people for directions before a horse-drawn cart stopped by us and offered a ride to wherever we wanted to go for a small fee. We agreed and asked the driver some questions along the way. This time, we inquired about anything strange. "Nah, can't recall 'nything more strange than the usual," he said to us. "Always newcomers passin' through. Some funny-lookin', some not. Just depends." We asked him to describe the 'funny-looking' visitors that the city has had recently but none of his descriptions really did us any good. According to his descriptions, even we would be considered 'funny-looking'.

The town hall was in the Political District at the southwest side of town. The mayor was out of the office for the day and wouldn't return until the next afternoon. We were ordered to deliver the message personally so we didn't let on that we had an urgent message for fear that a council member would force it from us. It was still fairly early in the evening so we decided to find the research center and get the times for the tours.

The Collegiate District was directly north over another enormous bridge. Each district was connected with huge bridges that could actually open up for ships to pass. When we made it into the district, we discovered that we were mispronouncing the word 'collegiate'. It was a word none of us had ever seen or heard before and we felt ignorant to be asking questions about it. Apparently, this city was home to something called a "college" where really smart people went to study and work with other really smart people. For what purpose, I didn't know. The research center wasn't difficult to find because the entire district was focused around it. The college and center were connected into one enormous building that had a glass dome on top of it. The building was actually larger than any church in the city and the town hall. It was a masterpiece of architecture and I would've been satisfied if looking at it from the outside was all I ever got to do.

The building was closed to the public for the day so we went and found the nearest inn. All of the inns in this district were much more expensive than we had hoped but we had the money and were pretty tired anyway so we decided to go along with it for the night. Once we had our rooms, we all split up to ask around about anything strange or suspicious.

Adam and I talked to almost a dozen different people, mostly people who seemed like travelers. Three people actually had information on the dark creatures. One guy had only heard rumors of shadow monsters swallowing people up and turning them into more monsters. Another girl claimed to have actually seen them. We asked her more but she didn't want to talk about it because it would only bring her more nightmares. Apparently a person close to her was turned into black smoke right before her eyes. The third person with information had also seen them and claimed to have come from a village that had been evacuated during an invasion of dark creatures. "It's a small village to the north, just to the west of Albaeta," he told us. "I was doing some business there when the guards came to us one night forcing everyone to leave for the city. Albaetian soldiers flooded into the streets to stem the attack but I don't know what happened after that. I hitched a ride with a man coming here." I was about to ask him more about the attack but Adam was more direct.

"What kind of business were you doing there?"

"I'm a researcher," he told us. "I work for the university here." He pulled out a book of notes to show us and flipped to some pages with his memories of the monsters. "I'm sorry I can't be of anymore help but so much happened in such a short amount of time that it's hard to recall."

"You've been more than enough help. Thank you." We parted ways with him to meet up with the rest of our group.

We all met at the fountain after an hour of gathering to pool our findings. Alice and Glinda had had the most luck out of the group. According to their sources, villages farther to the west have been completely overrun.

"One guy was terrified as he recalled his experiences. An entire town was swallowed in a single night, he said."

"We also had a couple girls say they lost their parents and brother to the shadows. They even saw their brother get turned into another creature and chase them." Dorothy and Eric only had one lead and it was just a story someone else had heard from another person about a city in the northwest that was recruiting people from the surrounding villages to combat the threat.

"So I guess these aren't just isolated events," I wondered. "It sounds like this is a country-wide threat," Dorothy remarked. I took out one of the more detailed country maps that we had come across and found a quill and ink in my bag. "Did anyone get any names of these places?" I asked. They gave me what they got and I marked it down with X's on the map for places that had been destroyed and O's for places that were at least privy to the attacks. After I was finished we all took a look to see if there was any sort of pattern.

"It looks like most of it is concentrated to the west and along major channels," Alice noted. "The only odd one out is Castelle, just north of our home."

"Unless the darkness was moving in from the north or northwest," Adam said, drawing a line with his finger from known areas towards Castelle.

"It's a possibility," I said. "We're still probably lacking boatloads of information."

"What Adam said would make sense, though, since a powerful leader was at Castelle. Maybe he was heading the front of an assault?" Glinda inquired.

"But it was the mayor of that particular city," Dorothy remarked. "Unless he was being possessed by some sort of darkness-army-military-leader." That wasn't a bad assumption, but none of our sources indicated anything happening in the northern regions of the country.

"Since we know so little, maybe we should sleep on it and see if we can gather anything from the East District tomorrow," I suggested, rolling up the map. It was getting close to sunset and we'd had a long day so I figured it was best to have another small meal and go to sleep early. I had the feeling that I wouldn't get a lot of sleep tonight anyway so I figured it would be best to allocate as much time to it as possible.

Chapter 14

The next morning, we made it to the earliest guided tour of the research facility. It turned out to be one of the most intriguing experiences I would ever have. People from all over the country and even from other parts of the world were working together behind big windows to make new discoveries. Classes were being taught in some rooms while animals and plants were being bred in others. We saw tools and equipment that none of us could have imagined in our wildest dreams. There was even an entire sector dedicated to the magical arts. While Alice was most excited about the nature studies, Dorothy was especially captivated by the work in what is called the Arcane Sector. Powerful mages from across the land were collaborating to discover new ways of casting spells. When I noticed that Dorothy wasn't with us halfway through the tour, I turned to find her fixated on one of the rooms. She also had a book out and was taking notes. I stifled a chuckle. Even whenever we were on a break she was still studying.

There was a kitchen and restaurant lounge attached between the college and the research center and our tickets allowed us a free meal so we had our lunch there. The whole time we ate, Dorothy was going over the notes she had taken. Alice was also taking the opportunity to write down everything she had learned from the tour before it faded from her memory. The meal was spectacular and we contemplated going back to the inn and napping before visiting the town hall. "How about we ask around here in the lounge while we have the time?" Glinda suggested. I was so full that I hadn't even thought of questioning anyone before our meeting with the mayor.

"That's a great idea," I said as I put a hand on my belly. "After I can get this settled down." Then there was a discussion about the meal we just had and laughs were shared about our bloated bellies.

We split back into our groups of two and fanned out across the room. Adam and I went straight back to the research center but were turned away since the tours were done. Expressing our reasoning to the guards didn't work and they informed us that the scientists inside were far too busy to be bothered with questions and that our best bet would be to visit the college. We took his advice and went to find a teacher or someone with that level of knowledge and experience to help us.

When we met back up, everyone had about the same amount of information to share as before. It was apparent that the people here really were quite busy and that the issues outside these walls stayed outside to everyone who did not make regular travels apart of their work.

"The best thing we could find was something about a quarantine at a small town near here," Eric told us.

"We heard something like that to," Alice concurred.

"Any details?" I asked them.

"Well, not really..." Glinda began.

"Apparently, a bunch of soldiers from this city and the capital evacuated a little town and have the place blocked off for some sort of special research that is being conducted by this center and the college," Alice explained.

"We didn't even get that much," Dorothy commented.

"Think we should fan out again and ask questions specifically relating to that?" Adam asked, looking at me. I checked the time on a large clock that hung between a pair of tall windows and determined it was time to head on over to the town hall.

"Maybe we can inquire the mayor about that directly," I suggested.

A soldier awaited us at the entrance to the Political District and escorted us directly into the town hall. We were a little early but so was the mayor so she called us in immediately. I ended up really liking her and kind of enjoying this meeting; she was a very direct and down-to-earth person.

"This may be hard to believe, but your reputation is beginning to precede you," she told us as we entered the chamber. "I'm not sure how you handle fame but given the circumstances I wouldn't say that is a particularly good thing." She had us take seats at two tables in front of her podium. I handed her the letter before I sat down. She opened it up and skimmed through for a moment before handing it to a councilman. "I generally try and avoid communication with that whale from Ruciam, but one can only do so much." I tried not to laugh and I heard Adam almost explode.

"I'm sorry that I have to do this but since you're here I need to send you on another mission... Well, I don't *need* to, but I want to." She gestured for a guard to bring out a large map that he then hung on the wall. "If you haven't already noticed, my city is big and popular. To avoid many problems that large cities bring, I enforce heavy regulations on the size and structure of my town. This has led to a handful of smaller villages popping up outside of our general boundaries." The guard used a stick to indicate these towns on the map. "One of these in particular, Guarrom, has succumbed to the darkness once again."

She noticed the puzzled expressions on our faces so she went off on a tangent. "Oh, right, you're young. This isn't the first time we've seen this threat. Eleven years ago, this country was attacked by shadow creatures that were thwarted after a one-year siege. A soldier from the capital with a shiny, magical sword sacrificed himself to drive them off." I could feel my teammates' gazes shift to me for a second. I felt a shock run down my spine but all I could do was gulp and listen. I'm not even sure I blinked again after she mentioned that.

"Anyway," the mayor started again. "Guarrom was once overrun by the darkness and turned into a forward-assault base by a leader of the darkness to attack this city and thus gain a direct route to the capital. It was not the only city that fell to this fate and many are still in ruins, mostly on the southern half of this continent. We thought we had cleared out the town after the shadows disappeared but it appears that they left it in a way that would allow them to easily retake it if need be and apparently, 'need be' is be right now." She paused to take a drink of water while we all soaked this unusual information in. Why had we never learned any of this? Perhaps it was a result of coming from a small, isolated village but something this huge should have at least partially reached our ears.

She continued, "we took careful steps to avoid a panic here. *Very* careful steps. As soon as the threat became apparent, we evacuated the city and sent in soldiers who were ultimately repelled. It was then that I called for aid from the capital and had the entire town sealed off. The darkness has been surprisingly cooperative and we rarely see any attacks to the perimeter which leads me to very seriously believe that they are preparing something. The sewer system here is being heavily monitored for underground threats but I need you to delve inside the village itself and uncover whatever they are plotting. Do not feel the need to kill everything or decapitate the monster in charge—we don't have the manpower readily available to save your asses."

A guard passed out pamphlets to each of us that contained the details of our mission. "I won't send you in alone," the mayor assured us. "A team of researchers from the Collegiate District will join your quest. They have already been briefed on the mission and have spent the last week preparing for it. They will know exactly what to look for and, in some cases, what to do if you have any questions. You all need to work together and take care of each other. This mission isn't just about protecting this city or saving a small village, it's about protecting the capital, this country, and defeating the darkness for good." Her words made me feel a little excited to be doing this. I felt more patriotic and even heroic that we were being tasked with such an important assignment but I was also extremely curious about the history of all this. Just more mysteries to be uncovered.

It was only a half-day's journey to Guarrom by horse but we were required to stay in Linareus for two more days while the researchers finished their preparations so we were actually pretty excited to finally get some work done. By this point in our overall quest, we couldn't stay sitting around for very long. Our bodies were becoming so accustomed to moving that being confined to city limits caused to get a little antsy.

The three researchers we had joining us were interesting characters. Two of them were women in their 30s and one was a man in his 40s. One of the ladies was actually a teacher at the college and she said she taught a subject called biology which was the study of living things. Out of everyone here, I think she was the most eager to visit this village. We tried to explain to her that these monsters weren't like anything living but she needed to see for herself how they functioned without being alive. Her theory was that the reason they attacked and swallowed humans was because of something inside them that craved to be alive again. After hearing that, Dorothy whispered to me that this woman thought way too much about some of this stuff.

Ever since our meeting with the mayor, my mind was full of thoughts about the history of this dark threat. She said a soldier with a magical sword had sacrificed himself to save the country and eliminate the enemy. Why hadn't any of us heard about this stuff? Had our parents and the other adults in town known of this and decided to keep it a secret? During our down time before this trip, we threw around ideas and wondered if my sword was the one from the story.

"If that's so, then you're, like, the chosen one to save us all again," Adam suggested. "Which means you may eventually have to sacrifice yourself. I hope you're prepared for that."

Alice smacked his arm and said, "don't even joke about stuff like that!"

As usual, most of the things we talked about were only speculations. It seemed, however, that every time we began to uncover one mystery, a dozen more popped up. We kept running into nothing but clues this whole time and I think it was beginning to wear on everyone. I was doing my best to put on a brave face but the constant flow of errands and the numerous questions were beginning to plague me. How on earth did the people before us deal with this threat? And what all had that knight done leading up to his sacrifice?

The cordon surrounding the village was happy to see us; the men and women watching the perimeter seemed weary and exhausted. We met with the captain in charge of the particular half of the circle that we arrived at and she gave us a quick rundown of what they had been going through each night and what to expect inside the town. "Every night we get hit with small groups of shadow creatures but so far there hasn't been a major assault which is why we believe they are preparing for something. We've sent people to investigate during the day but none ever return. As you can see, there are clouds hanging above the town; they don't go away."

We had a quick lunch while receiving all the information we might need before making our way into the city. The older researcher suggested we hang back and check things along the perimeter but the other two were eager to get inside the village and see what we can get done before sunset. We only had so many hours to gather as much intel as possible, one of the ladies said.

The town itself didn't seem to be much different than our hometown. The only real difference was the style of the buildings but as far as size and layout went it felt much like Valencia. Even though it was early in the afternoon, the overcast above us blanketed everything in a dull, gray color which caused the shadows inside the buildings and around corners to be darker.

"We need to search for bodies," the teacher said as she made her way to an open doorway.

"Wait!" I shouted as she went right inside. We all followed after her, concerned for her safety inside the dark building and then found her dragging a body into the dim light of the doorway.

"Give me a light," she said as she began examining the body. The other two joined her while Glinda generated some pixies to hover around them.

"You can't just go running off like that," Adam told her. "It's dangerous." She didn't say a word while she worked.

There was only one lifeless body in the first building. The next building housed two and the following building contained three. We were seeing an obvious pattern as we continued but, at the fourth building, things changed a little bit. There were four bodies, as we expected, but this time they were each missing a different body part. We saw this again in the fifth building. None of the researchers said anything to us during this time so Dorothy finally spoke up outside the sixth building.

"Have you discovered anything that you aren't sharing with us?" She had a more frustrated tone in her voice than usual. They looked at each other and the oldest one finally told us that they really only made one legitimate discovery:

"All of these bodies are real, dead villagers, but not a single one has shown any signs of stiffness or decay.

It is as if they died very recently and the ones missing limbs lack any sort of bodily fluids. All of it is rather baffling so we just figure we'll keep going until we get another clue." Dorothy was irritated that they had so little information after all this time. We hadn't been asked to do a single thing so we'd really just been following them around and providing security that didn't seem to be needed. Everything was so quiet and still.

Eventually, we found ourselves in the town square at the center. The researchers were eager to visit the hall so we went there first. Inside was the most chilling scene thus far which entirely changed our mood about this mission.

The hall was, surprisingly, full. Full of humans, no different than us. Every body was sitting in a chair at a table all facing a council at the front of the room. Every body was sitting upright with their eyes forward. Every body was completely motionless. We opened the door and walked in with hesitation but not a single one turned to look at us.

I felt a shock of surprise in my chest when I saw the room filled with civilization. The researchers went to them to ask questions but none replied to their inquiries. They just continued staring, motionless, to the front of the room.

Alice pressed on the shoulder of one man causing him to fall forward, bonking his head on the desk. "Um…" she began. "These people aren't alive."

Glinda squeaked and yanked her hand back after she touched another one that also fell forward which confirmed Alice's theory. My heartbeat picked up. "Is the sun setting already?" Adam asked, looking out the window at the fading glow in the cloud cover. "Let's get back to the cordon," I demanded.

None of us made it through the doorway before we heard wood scraping against the floor. I turned around to see chairs being pushed back from the tables. The bodies were moving. I wanted to shout another command but my voice got caught in my throat. The people rose up and turned to face us. Their eyes still didn't blink and their bodies slouched slightly as if it took a sufficient effort to support themselves.

"Run!" Dorothy shouted as she raised a thin wall of fire between us and the advancing horde. We bolted out of the town hall to see more and more reanimated bodies lurching out of the buildings. They were all of the bodies that had been inspected and more.

We continued to run back the way we came as bodies sluggishly exited each building to our right and left. Great cautious was used to not land any mortal blows and only knock them back. "They're being possessed just like the townsfolk back at Castelle!" Alice shouted. "I thought you guys said they were dead?" Dorothy asked the researchers.

159

"They were when we inspected them!" The male researcher said, dodging a swipe at his head.

"If that's the case then…" Dorothy said as she fired two magic missiles that ripped the legs off a villager.

"What are you doing?!" I shouted at her.

"They're dead!" She snapped back. "There's no sense in preserving their corpses in exchange for our own!"

I didn't like the idea of brutally attacking humans but I guess they left me no choice. I gritted my teeth and split one in half at the waist. I was reminded of what happened back at Castelle and how we had to fight for our lives against the possessed villagers. I still had nightmares about it. This felt different, though. These people weren't acting the same way at all. Before, our enemies were attacking us with weapons and an immense ferocity. These people, on the other hand, just seemed… defenseless. Helpless. They had no weapons and were just stumbling after us. I could almost feel the rage in the villagers at Castelle but the villagers here seemed completely emotionless, like there wasn't any form of life within them anymore. It felt almost senseless to destroy them… they really were already dead.

We were forced to show no mercy towards the bodies in our way. Glinda disapproved most of all and actually stopped at one point to vomit next to some barrels. She was usually so good at keeping her composure in the face of danger but this was different. I could understand her struggle–I noticed how each of us would hesitate or hold back at times. This felt too much like murder and it was making us uneasy. Even being assured they were already dead didn't make this feel any better. I couldn't put my finger on exactly why it bothered me so much to fight them.

Before we could even make it to the gate we saw figures moving toward us in the distance. "Reinforcements!" the head researcher shouted. "We're saved!" The glint of body armor and drawn swords did indeed indicate that soldiers, probably from the cordon, were moving in through the gate. Something about their movements looked peculiar, though. I guess Dorothy noticed the same thing I did because two fireballs whizzed past my head and exploded in the middle of the advancing group. "Why did you do that?" the male researcher yelled at her.

"They're possessed or dead, just like these poor fools!" Dorothy replied as she fired a magic missile through the skull of a zombie that had grabbed ahold of Eric's shoulders.

"It looks like we're all alone," Adam said anonymously.

"We're not alone!" I exclaimed. "We're all still alive and these beasts are clearly no match for us! We WILL make it out of here alive!"

Alice suggested we cut through a building to our left since more and more of what we began referring to as zombies crowded around us. She was right, we had to keep moving if we were going to find a way out of here. The building seemed to have been a huge general store in the past so it provided a lot of obstacles for us to leave behind.

Coming out of the back entrance, we spotted more movement to our right so we took a left and made our way back towards the city center. The zombies were dumb and didn't consider flanking us or blocking a path. All that seemed to matter was chasing us.

There was a large building in the distance that rivaled the town hall in size. "Let's try there!" I shouted as we plowed through a small group of townsfolk. I didn't think much about the next step, I just knew that funneling through a big building might help put some distance between us and the majority of these zombified people.

The building seemed to be a former military barracks and was mostly empty. We were grateful that it wasn't filled with armed zombie soldiers and the few we encountered weren't wielding weapons so we made quick work of them. Eventually, we found ourselves in a large courtyard at the center that seemed to have been used for combat training in the past. Practice dummies and equipment were scattered about.

"Which way now?" One of the researchers asked as we looking around at the various doorways lining the walls.

The only pathway left for you.... is to hell. The dark, familiar voice came to us from all directions. As quickly as a chill could run down my spine, the torches around the doorways flared up with purple and black flames.

"You again?!" Adam shouted.

I finally found you again, the voice said with a chuckle. Alice used her magic to bust the rock walls that held the torches but as they fell the fire shot towards us, danced around while we took swings at it, and then combined together to form a ball of fire in front of us.

"Black fire! It's demonic!" The male researcher commented.

"Demonic? I knew it felt dark and strange," Dorothy said, not taking her gaze off the floating fire as it formed itself into the shape of a man larger than Eric.

It said nothing to us as we felt the flames got hotter. "It's going to attack!" Dorothy warned just before its two arms burst forward at us. Glinda reacted quickly and raised her hand up to create a barrier of light in between us and the fire. Her shield caused the flames to spit in two and explode at two corners of the courtyard behind us.

Noticing what Glinda's simple light screen was able to do, I got the idea to take advantage of the short lull. I darted forward with my sword, raising it high, and brought it down at the chest of the monster. The flames were so hot and they licked at my forearms as my blade connected. I shouted in pain but didn't pull back until my sword cut clean through. My target yelled in pain, drowning out my own scream. I pulled back to my team and commanded them to run for it. I took an extra second to make sure the beast wasn't preparing to follow before I joined them through a doorway to the left.

The passage we chose wasn't the best decision on our part; there were many intersections and we found ourselves lost almost immediately. But, then again, we had no idea where we were going from the beginning, so it could be said that we were never actually 'lost'.

"Let me see your arms," Glinda said to me as we rounded another turn. "They're alright," I said. "You can look at them when we stop." Once again, I was lying to keep her from worrying. In all reality, I could still feel them burning. It was as if the fire was still crawling across my skin and eating their way towards my bones.

"Up ahead!" Alice shouted from the front. I saw ahead of us a dark gray hue, indicating an open doorway to the outside. We finally found some freedom to make our way to real safety away from this forsaken town.

Bringing up the rear, I was the last one to see what happened after I heard a sharp squeal. When I emerged from the building, I saw the team fighting furiously to cut through a dense pack of zombies. The squeal was still ongoing and I finally recognized that it belonged to Alice. To our right I could see her wrapped up in the arms of two very fat zombies. She was panicking as they carried her away, separating themselves from the horde attacking us.

Adam had gone into a mad rage to clear a path out. He was dumping all the magic he had in his veins to hasten his arms and increase the power in each swing. I don't know if it was because he was moving so fast but I thought I noticed a red tint of energy radiating from his body.

I joined in the fray by attacking the zombies coming from our left to keep Adam from getting hit from behind. Glinda had launched pixies at the retreating behemoths but I couldn't see if they had any sort of success. Alice eventually stopped screaming which sent Adam further off the edge.

I turned around just in time to see him doing something new. He was doing to his whole body what he normally does with his swords: spinning. He had both swords out and was using what magic he had left in him, more than I originally thought, to twirl like violent whirlwind, ripping zombies to pieces all around him. He somehow managed to maintain his sense of direction because he was slowly stepping in the direction that Alice was taken and leaving a wide, bloody trail behind him.

Glinda and I were guarding the rear of our group while Dorothy and Eric protected the researchers as they called out stray zombies. We couldn't follow Adam with the numbers that were piling up around us. I mentioned that to Glinda and she didn't hesitate to address the issue.

She began powering up light magic in her hands and eventually commanded all of us to run towards Adam. We did and she erected a light screen in front of the zombies that were circling all around us. We now had a window of opportunity to catch up. Once we did, however, we realized we weren't needed. Adam had already exited the swarm of enemies and was taking a left down the alleyway that I assumed, and hoped, was the right way.

We sprinted after him, closing the gap quickly. Dorothy let loose a barrage of fireballs at the trailing zombies that exploded on impact. As we turned the corner, I realized that my heart was beating out of my chest. The prolonged fighting and sprinting was something my body never seemed to adjust to and the burn marks on my arms had grown in size and were now eating their way up past my elbows. I tried to ignore them; there was no time to worry about a small, manageable injury.

When we turned a corner we found Adam engaged with a handful of tall shadow monsters. They were eerie looking and quite a bit different than what we'd seen before, but closely resembled creatures we'd fought in Ruciam. They all had long, thin limbs, bright glowing eyes, and didn't show any fear of the light, either.

Adam was outmatched. Their long arms could dart around him and his swords with ease. Dorothy had begun firing magic missiles immediately and Glinda followed with pixies to heal him. By the time we arrived he had already received a number of cuts. Eric went straight after one, knocking it down and then turning fully to bat away another with his spear. I powered up my blade, causing it to glow brightly, and slashed one straight down the middle.

I went on to stab at another but before my blade could connect, an arm came from around me and tied itself around my forearm causing the burns to sting worse. Another arm wrapped around my midsection and lifted me high into the air, upside down. Before it slammed me to the ground I saw that the beast I had just split in two was now operating as two separate bodies.

Hitting the cobblestone ground hurt more than I imagined it would. The wind was knocked completely out of me and for a second or two my vision seemed to click off. I was delirious trying to roll over and push myself up. My sword wasn't in my hand anymore and my fuzzy vision didn't allow me to find it quickly. Then my body warmed up. Warmer and warmer. My vision returned and all the pain went away. My lungs filled up with air and that's when I noticed Glinda's light engulfing me. I found my sword nearby and charged at the two halves of my enemy.

Adam was tiring himself out. I think Eric noticed, too, because he stayed nearby. While Adam was doing an amazing job at eliminating our enemies, the strain was taking a toll on his body–he had never operated at such a high level before. None of us three guys didn't have a large supply of magic power to begin with so it was a wonder how he was still standing.

These creatures seemed smarter than any other we had encountered before and they also noticed when Adam began to slow down. I had just finished off one when I saw Adam take a swing and miss. The beast darted to the right to avoid his sword and brought its arm all the way around Adam's body. Eric was quicker and slashed the arm with his spear but the dangerous, clawed part stayed its course right toward Adam's back.

It seemed to happen in slow motion. Razor-like claws ripped their way into my best friend's lower-back. I heard someone scream, Glinda I think, but it sounded like an echo far away. In a flash of light, Dorothy was by Adam's side as he fell. She had fireballs orbiting her body and sending them to explode on the monsters all around. The pixies around us were immediately on Adam to try and save him.

Was this really happening? Was my best friend dying in an alleyway far from home? We were brought here on some quest for someone else and didn't know why or where we were going. The girl he cared for most wasn't even around to say goodbye. So why? Why was this happening here and now?

Blood was pouring from his back and mouth in record amounts. Glinda was beside him and eventually the light from her and her pixies blocked out his body. I was lost. My own body was completely frozen and all I could do was watch my best friend die. My brain wasn't even processing the events unfolding before my eyes. I was numb.

"Phillip!" Dorothy's voice broke my trance. I looked up to see her shooting icy missiles that flew past my head. I turned to see the being of black and purple flames rounding the corner behind us. "Get your ass in gear!" She shouted at me as she spun around and knocked another dark creature off its feet with a spell.

At this point, I was furious. *I. Am. So. Sick and tired. Of this stupid shit.* I thought as I gritted my teeth and powered up my sword. The demon was closing in and I was ready to make him and everything else go away. I wasn't even thinking about vengeance for my best friend, I just wanted all of this to end so I could go home and see my family and not worry anymore. I wanted all of this to end so no more bad would happen to us or anyone else. I wanted my friends and I to be safe and happy once again.

I raised my sword above my head, increasing the power as he closed in on me. I was ready to strike until he pulled back at the last moment and began generating fireballs in each hand. He was just out of reach, but I didn't care. I was going to strike him and and make all this disappear. I took a step forward and dropped my sword toward his head. He moved back, farther out of reach, but that somehow didn't save him. The white light enveloping my blade had elongated itself enough to split my enemy right down the middle.

My blade ripped my target in half and even took out much of the cobblestone ground in the way and cracked the walls of the surrounding buildings. I pulled my sword back and then cut him into more and more pieces. Then I turned my sights on the monsters that were engaged with my friends.

A creature had given Eric an uppercut that put him to the ground. As he struggled to get up, Dorothy moved in the way and was dancing her hands through the air to create enough spells that could keep the beasts at bay until Eric made it back to his feet. I couldn't make it quick enough to stop a claw from ripping into Dorothy so I tried to do a throw attack like Adam had always done but, at the last second, something told me not to let go of my hilt. I'm not sure what that feeling was or where it came from but I obeyed and then watched as a flash of light separated from the magic around my blade and slashed through two monsters.

I swung my blade through the air a couple more times, testing the new attack, and found that it worked whenever I wanted it to. Arcs of energy erupted from the tip of my blade and ripped apart every one of the creatures that remained. This time, the pieces didn't stand back up. I wondered if the light magic of my weapon caused them to really die for good. I hoped that was the case. The pieces eventually dissolved into the air, confirming my theory.

"Wow," a familiar male voice said. I was still in a rage-fueled trance so I couldn't quite pinpoint the owner but I knew I recognized it.

"You're alive?!" I shouted as I turned to my right.

"Yeah, we're just fine," the male researcher said as him and the two women stepped from a doorway. "We ducked in here while you were fighting. A small shadow creature popped out at us but we worked together and I think we killed it." I wanted to be glad that they were okay, but I had really thought it was Adam at first. I felt the weight of the whole world fall on me. How could I have let this happen? *Because you're a failure.*

Dorothy and Eric were being treated by Glinda so I joined them to heal my own wounds, too, and ask the question I wasn't sure if I wanted an answer to. For a while I stood by and stared at the ground as Glinda did her work.

"What's wrong with you?" Dorothy asked me, stretching her repaired arms.

"Are you serious?" I asked her. "How can you even say that!" She just stared at me and then pointed past me to where I had left the researchers. I turned and saw Adam standing there talking to them. He looked over at me and said, "are you guys ready yet? We're in a hurry!"

Chapter 15

It wasn't long before we saw the northeastern edge of town.

"How can we even be sure we're going the right way?" Glinda questioned.

"We know we're going the right direction because obstacles keep confronting us," I told her as I kicked the leg out from under a shadow creature so Adam could split it in half at the waist. Since we had healed up we hadn't had more than thirty seconds of a break. We hadn't run into anymore of the tall, rubbery-like beasts but there was no end to the little guys that we were used to dealing with.

We kind of had an idea where we were going because the big guys that took Alice were so wide and heavy that they left a trail in their wake. Cracked stones and broken benches or carts lined a road leading out of town. One of the female researchers informed us that we were heading out of town in the direction of another small village.

We hadn't even made it to the edge of the city before we came under another major threat. It hadn't been fifteen minutes since I defeated the fiery demon and we were now dodging a rain of purple and black fireballs. I turned to see the demon racing after us, floating through the air and leaving a trail of fire behind.

"Will anything stop this guy?" I shouted.

"The next village is only a couple miles away but I'm not sure if we'll make it," one of the female researchers said.

"Glinda, do you think you can distract him?" I asked. She said she'd try her best and then released scores of pixies before setting up a transparent screen that stretched across the road.

Adam Eric, and I had to carry the researchers because they didn't have the magical capacity to energize themselves to make themselves run for extended periods of time. We were all getting pretty low on power at this point but it didn't take much for us to fuel our muscles enough to go a couple miles.

The adjacent town wasn't much different than the last; it seemed mostly like a housing district with a few shopping areas. One of the fat zombies that kidnapped Alice waited for us at the entrance which told us we weren't wrong to come here. This time I actually got a good look at it. It was a zombified human, alright, but it was filled to the brim with dark energy. The entire body was bloated and brimming with shadow magic. It was a disgusting construct that looked like it had been pieced together with multiple human body parts, including four arms. "I guess this explains the missing pieces of the bodies we found earlier," Dorothy said.

All that dark energy made it physically stronger than foes we had grown accustomed to. Eric swung his spear at the head but the beast caught it, lifted the spear, and Eric, up into the air, and threw both with ease at Adam who was charging in. I powered up my blade again, ready to pop the belly with my new attack. Before I could swing, the monster sensed the buildup of energy and coughed out a shadowball spell that exploded at my chest and sent me flying backward.

"Hurry!" the male researcher shouted. "I can see flames in the distance!" I believed he was referring to the demon that had been hunting us. It was a strange feeling to become the hunted while we were also hunting. When I sat up, I witnessed Dorothy releasing a slew of magical missiles at the beast's stomach. The spells were like sharp darts so I figured she was trying to pop the belly as I had attempted before but her efforts seemed to have no effect.

As I charged the beast, Eric was ahead of me and using his magic to propel his spear at the open belly while Adam distracted it. Glinda had pixies orbiting the beast's head and they kept zapping it all over with little light spells. Eric's spear struck dead center and actually seemed to go in halfway only to be bounced right back out. "Its... unbreakable," he said.

It was a wonder how the thing could move while it was so full. That was when I got an idea. "Dorothy, Glinda!" I shouted to them as I tried to cut off the left hand. "See if you can fill it up and pop it from the inside!" The girls caught on quick and reacted immediately. Glinda created a constant flow of pixies and sent them down the monster's throat. The beast choked them down and squeezed at his own throat to stop them. Dorothy put out both hands and fed magical energy in with the pixies and pushed out on the walls of his throat to allow more to enter.

It didn't take much longer before the creature's stomach expanded. It continued to get bigger as the girls drained their magic pools. "Let's go!" Adam shouted to Eric and I. The three of us took advantage of the lull in attacks and unloaded on the enlarging belly. Eventually, Eric noticed the outer layers of skin rip apart and called for us to retreat. Glinda created a few dozen more pixies and sent them in before we all ran for the nearest doorway. Just before entering the building, I caught a glimmer of fire burning through the trees on the outskirts of the village.

Instead of going back out the same doorway, we continued through the building to exit into an alleyway. An enormous explosion rang out and the force of it caused the building to shake before we made it out. Some members of the team even lost their footing for a moment during the tremor. Hopefully that would provide a decent distraction for the demon chasing us.

Making our way through the town was a lot easier after that. There wasn't a single shadow creature to confront us as we searched for clues to the location of our friend. A hole busted completely through one building invited us to try looking there first. It led us down another road until we found a broken side of a building next to an alleyway as if something had had trouble fitting through. I made sure to take a look behind us before going into the alley and saw smoke and a faint glow of fire at the other end of town. The demon was probably burning down buildings searching for us.

We were led to a large church. The grass surrounding the building had grown tall and vines covered so much of the outside that it was hard to tell that it was made of red brick and not just plants. It was odd because this building seemed to not have received any sort of maintenance in years while the rest of the village looked like it had been kept clean until quite recently.

Entering the church was a slight challenge due to the thick vegetation that covered all around and even into the building itself. A hole in the floor near the pulpit became our target. Sneaking in wasn't an option due to the creaking floorboards. It was darker in here and the girls didn't have a lot of magic to spare creating a bunch of lights.

We didn't even come close to the hole before another fat monster climbed out to confront us. Adam was quick, though, and made a slash at one hand, separating the fingers from the palm. The beast screamed and belched a shadowball spell that sent him across the room and into the wall.

Eric and I charged the monster only to be swept aside together by one arm. Dorothy and Glinda used the same strategy as before. It was a dangerous move on their part because they had used so much to defeat the last one after using up quite a bit in the last village. I urged them not to but they kept up their work. "Why don't you help us then?" Dorothy suggested kind of hatefully, as if I hadn't ever helped them before. She must be more irritable than usual from the draining and exhaustion.

I knew I had the capacity for spellcasting now, but it had always been with my blade. I still didn't know how to manipulate magic and weave spells or do anything that the girls can do. "Phillip!" Glinda shouted. I decided to give it a shot, like I had been doing all this time with my new weapon. The two girls were running dangerously low and I think the monster knew it. He had been taking steps toward them, gulping down their efforts like drinking water.

I joined them, pointed my sword at his mouth, and powered up my blade. I wasn't sure exactly what to do so I imagined releasing my magic, like I had done with attacks earlier, down his throat. I focused on making it a constant stream and not a burst this time. The magic around my blade fluctuated for a little bit as I worked in my mind what it needed to do. The monster was almost within arm's length of us by now. I only had seconds left to spare. My weapon still wasn't doing what I wanted to do so I screamed at it in my head to just do what I say and make it happen. Finally, it acted, and bright, white energy shot from the sword and into the mouth of the beast.

The beam of light resembled a thick, sparkling mist as it covered the entire opening. The creature's eyes widened all the way as it began to choke. It tried the same tactic as the last one to squeeze his throat shut but to no avail. The girls stopped their work as mine began. I guess they could sense it better than I could of what was happening.

As the beast neared the point of exploding, I tried to shut off the stream but I couldn't figure out how. It was pouring out of my blade at this point like a river. I was afraid it would run dry but I didn't feel as if hardly any of it was being used at all, like there was some unlimited supply. I began to get very nervous as the beast expanded more and more, well beyond the point of the last one.

My friends urged me to shut it off but I told them I didn't know how. I asked Dorothy how to make it stop but she seemed surprised that I didn't have any clue of what to do. Finally, Eric just grabbed me around the waist and carried me over to the hole in the ground where we all dove in just before the monster exploded.

We found ourselves at the beginning of a tunnel that stretched on for an unknown distance. As we got to our feet and our ears stopped ringing, Glinda conjured up a couple pixies to scout ahead for us. "I guess you don't need us anymore, do you, Chosen One?" Adam said to me, patting my back and walking down the pathway. He said it in a tone that made me wonder if he was really joking. "He's just tired," Eric assured me. "Good work up there."

One pixie eventually came back to us while the other kept going. The tunnel must've ran all the way across town. Tired and nearly empty on power, our chase was slowed from a run to a brisk pace. By now, all that kept us moving even remotely quickly was the anticipation of seeing or friend again. Adam was up ahead taking bigger strides than the rest of us. I moved quicker to catch up to him.

"Hey, how ya feeling?" I asked, concerned about the amount of energy he's dumped out so far. "Not well and I won't feel right until we rescue our friend," he told me with a frustrated tone, as if I had asked the dumbest question. I decided to just leave it at that. I could tell by his movements that he was past the point of exhaustion. We all knew how much him and Alice cared for each other even if they never spoke about it.

The pixie that went on ahead found another pathway to the right and waited on us to get close before flying down it. The new way was considerably shorter and took us to an enormous room. But before we even made it to the room we found ourselves swatting away an assortment of vegetation that grew from the ground, walls, and ceiling. "Alice was definitely here," Dorothy told us. We had to chop our way through a gauntlet of thick, thorny vines and brambles before we entered the chamber.

Countless brambles, vines, and other plants covered every inch of this room that was easily twice the size of the town hall we were in earlier tonight. Fire was slowly burning away plants and small trees throughout the room creating the only light source. At the opposite end of the room, suspended in the air, was a large ball made up of the same plants that sparkled with green magic.

Standing in the center of the chamber and facing the ball was a man. A very well-dressed and fat man. When he turned to face us, I noticed he was ugly and sweaty and dressed like some important council member from the cities we've visited. In his left hand was Alice's staff.

"Good evening," he said to us with both arms out as if welcoming us to a party. "I am the mayor of Guarrom. Welcome." Another mayor? This was kind of annoying. Adam wasn't waiting for questions or answers, though. A spinning sword was sent flying at our new enemy only to be swatted away with one hand of dark magic.

I heard Dorothy sigh and then say, "what's the deal with mayors?" The man just laughed and said, "well, it goes back to our first invasion of this country. Originally, generals, such as myself, led large armies through the night. That proved unsuccessful, obviously, so this time we decided to take another route by possessing townspeople and what better townspeople than leaders of the masses! So far, we've made great strides. Although, many of these human bodies are weak and feeble. I cannot wait until we rid the world of your filth."

"Where's Alice?!" Adam yelled, raising his other weapon. "And why did you kidnap her?" The man turned to look at the sphere hanging from the wall before answering. "She's shut herself in that cocoon. Before exhausting all of her magical energy and passing out, she killed every one of my soldiers and sealed herself away. A remarkable young lady, if I do say so myself."

To answer your other question," he began has he turned back to us. "Kidnapping her was an accident. You see, the last time we were here, that sword of yours, young man, was quite a nuisance. One of my missions now is to kill you and make it go away. However, my idiot minions grabbed the wrong person and now here we are." He pointed at my sword as he spoke. My heart raced faster when he said those words.

He apparently had a part in the story of my weapon's history and I wanted to gather more information but Adam was more focused on the present. Another spinning sword attack was sent towards the possessed mayor while magic was used to draw the other one from the ground and return to it's owner's hand. The enemy blocked the second ranged attack the same way as the last but Adam closed in quickly to make an attempt at stabbing the man in the gut.

Adam's target blocked the attack, but two of Dorothy's icy shards closed in from each side. Eric and Glinda both flew past me before my brain clicked into action. Once again, everyone was way ahead of me. I powered up my sword and ran forward to join the frenzy.

Dorothy and Adam were both attacking furiously. I noticed, though, that Adam didn't seem to have any magic backing up the swings of his swords. He must be using anything he has left just to make his body function the right way. Dorothy was also clearly holding back. She was casting spells as quickly and intensely as she normally would but each spell looked about half the size as usual. Eric and Glinda weren't performing much differently, either. We were all tired. I knew that my sword could put out immense amounts of power, but the only way I knew to harness it was to release it from the blade; it wasn't like I could empower my own body with the magic that came from my sword.

As I charged forward with my powered-up blade, I felt my joints pop and a sharp pain run through the side of my head. My body was also worn down. I guess I'd been using my weapon as extensively as possible without realizing or considering the toll it could have on my body. It made me wonder if I was even ready to wield this sword.

So many thoughts rushed through my head as I closed in on the mayor. I had to cut to the right because Eric took a step back to get in some wide swings with his spear. It was then that my eyes glanced up at the cocoon not far away. I wondered if I could check on Alice since the others seemed to be holding their own just fine.

I ran towards Alice's cage and swung my blade a few times, releasing magical slices at the thick brambles. When I was close enough, I used what little of my own magic I had in me to help myself jump high enough to cut away more of the cocoon.

I didn't get through enough to even see her before I came back to the ground but I had plenty left in me to make another jump or two. As I propelled myself into the air once more, a shadowball spell struck me in the back and sent me into the wall. I had no magic protecting my body and I was already sore to begin with so the blast hurt quite a bit, more than any other I'd been hit with before but I blamed it on my current state and not the mayor's power. I didn't want to give him any kind of credit. If that wasn't bad enough, I got caught up in the vines and brambles hanging from the wall and lost my sword.

I wondered how he found the time to hit me with a spell but, when I looked up, I got my answer. The two girls were behind a screen that Glinda had raised. Dorothy was firing spells from one side while Glinda was at the other, casting healing spells. The screen was covered in cracks and I figured it would be ready to shatter at any moment. Eric was at least ten feet away from the mayor and climbing to his feet. Adam, on the other hand, was at the biggest disadvantage of all. There wasn't a sword in either hand but he was still charging in with fists clenched. All the fighting that him and Eric had done in the past paid off because Adam was able to dodge each incoming swing and land a number of punches.

I worked on finding my weapon and freeing myself before getting too focused on their work. I didn't see my sword so I focused on making it appear in my hand. I had to clear the haze from my brain left over from the impacts that led me here but I eventually had my weapon back and was able to cut myself free.

After I landed on the floor I decided to keep my feet firmly planted there from now on and just use up whatever magic the sword had left in it. I moved to a position where I could focus on Alice but still catch the battle on my left peripheral.

I unleashed a slew of magical slashes after the cocoon but the thing was thick and strong. Each swing also released a sting of pain in my head but I did my best to ignore it all. I kept at it, avoiding another shadowball that exploded on the wall next to me, until I finally saw Alice unconscious inside. Just to be safe, I jumped up to her and cut her down directly and jumped back to the ground, barely avoiding another shadowball.

After I landed, I saw two more spells come at me so I ducked and weaved my way past them. The mayor had knocked everyone else back and now his sights were set on me. I laid Alice down and had my sword ready just in time to deflect another two spells. I then fired off at least a dozen consecutive energy slashes at him. Halfway through my onslaught, I got another splitting headache. I still felt like there was an unlimited amount of magic coming from my sword but my body was nearly done trying to harness all of it.

I shouted for Glinda to tend to Alice but she was busy casting a healing spell on Eric as he charged, without his spear, at the mayor who was focused on protecting himself from my attacks.

After I finished releasing a series of slashes at the mayor I decided to rush him, figuring it would help conserve whatever strength my body had left since I was hurting pretty badly from using my sword's magic. During my charge, I finally noticed the burns on my arms again and nearly dropped my sword. *Not this time! You're not going to let anyone down this time!*

Glinda released a couple pixies to hover around us as she ran over to check on Alice. Both new pixies flew to Dorothy first since she just got struck by a shadowball and was sent across the room. She wasn't moving when they arrived. Us guys had to be careful because only one pixie remained with us once the mayor struck one out of the air.

Adam had recovered one sword from the thick grass on the battlefield and Eric was still unarmed but going toe-to-toe with this mayor. I joined the fray and chopped down at our enemy but he dodged it and backhanded Adam into Eric. I swung a few more times only to give the mayor an opening to hit my chest and send me into the air.

As I came back down I saw the mayor powering up dark energy around his leg to give me a thunderous kick. I began to power up my sword but the headache came back and cut my concentration. A second before contact was made, Eric grabbed the powered leg with both hands and pulled it back. The mayor immediately caused the magic to explode and send both Eric and I across the room.

I landed hard and rolled a few times. My face was in the ground but I couldn't even find the strength to roll onto my back. I overheard Adam engaging the mayor and I honestly hoped he'd land the killing blow, otherwise we'd be done. Just as I was really losing hope, I heard the flutter of tiny wings above me. A pixie had come to my rescue.

The little bit of healing from the pixie was enough to get me to my feet. I was excited to see Dorothy back in motion and supporting Adam. The mayor obviously had the upper-hand over Adam but Dorothy's little onslaught of spells were enough to keep the battle going.

I didn't want to seem weak since they'd really been fighting more than me tonight so I ignored the pain running through my entire body and dragged myself back into the battle. My arms and legs felt like weights were attached to them but I kept pushing myself. It took so much effort and I wasn't exactly sure what kept me going at this point. The pixie was still mending my wounds which may have been the only reason I hadn't yet passed out, unlike Eric who was still hidden in the vegetation.

I started to power up my blade just a little bit when a searing pain ripped through my arm and caused me to drop it. I looked to see the burns from earlier. I kept forgetting about them but they had been creeping up both arms this whole time. The one on my right arm was reaching up onto my shoulder. *I don't have time for this*! I said to myself. "Can you do something about this?" I asked the pixie. It tried healing the burns directly but to no avail. It seemed awfully disappointed that it couldn't help. The poor thing was so cute that I cracked a little smile and said, "don't worry about it. It doesn't hurt. Why don't you go help Eric out?" It gave me a little smile and flew over to join its companion who was already attending to our unconscious teammate. As soon as its eyes were off me, I picked my sword back up and sluggishly moved into action.

Once I got by Adam's side and got into the groove of fighting, I kind of forgot about much of the pain I was in. "What's wrong with you, hero?" Adam said to me as we danced around our enemy.

"I was going to ask you the same thing! Don't you have a girl to protect? You're doing a bad job of impressing her!" I was under the impression we were making playful banter but he was serious.

"That's what all of us are doing, you idiot," he replied with an angry tone. "I meant why are you holding back? You have the key to winning fights like this, don't you? Hurry up before one of us is killed!" He seemed pretty mad about my weakness but there really wasn't much I could do about it; I was already maxing myself out.

Adam's words were enough to set me off and power my blade back up a little more than before. I thought my head was going to explode and my arm would fall off but I took the risk and swung. The mayor put out both hands and created a quick barrier of smoky shadow magic. He had a lot more power in his defense than I did in my attack so most of it was lost in a small explosion but I managed to rip his left arm from the shoulder down to his wrist and take off two fingers.

Not a drop of blood was spilt from the possessed body but he still felt plenty of pain. He was furious now and stomped a foot hard into the ground which created a smoky blast wave that sent Adam and I flying back. Dorothy tried to take advantage of the moment with a heavy fireball to the head but he just caught it and threw it back at her where it exploded at her feet.

The blast wave I was hit with wasn't too strong so I was able to just barely land on my feet while sliding a little ways. I noticed that Eric was back on his feet and had found his spear but the mayor also saw him moving and sent three shadowballs right after him. Eric was able to stop two but the third put him back to the ground.

The mayor now had nobody directly confronting him so he began readying another spell. He started by powering up shadow magic in his palms that grew to cover both hands. Gusts of wind came from the center of the room where he stood. The energy radiating from him caused a chill to run down my spine. None of us had the strength to stop this new attack.

He was still preparing his attack while looking around at the four of us. I had no idea if he was choosing a target or if this attack would wipe us all out at once. He had a smile on his face as he moved his gaze between each of us.

In the middle of his almost boastful display of power, however, he was abruptly halted. A number of thick brambles shot from the ground and wrapped around his arms and legs before moving around to the rest of his body. He attempted to rip them apart but only got a few before green magic began coursing through them as more and more glowing brambles appeared to attack him.

I looked over at the other end of the room to see Alice walking towards her target with both hands dancing around to control all of her plants. Glinda was unconscious and sitting up against the wall as a green light flowed over her body. She must've completely exhausted herself fixing Alice up who then began returning the favor.

The mayor was going all out to destroy the plants attacking him and send spells at his new enemy but she seemed to have fully recovered and had a plethora of assets filling the cavern. Nearly all of the vegetation she had conjured before was alive and well and ready to do her bidding.

The thorns on her plants ripped through skin to bury themselves deep inside. It wasn't long before Alice actually had vines running throughout the mayor's possessed body. She obviously had no inclination of preserving the physical remains of the former politician.

From within the body, dark magic erupted to fight away the threat but not enough energy remained. It was then that I saw Alice do something new: drain away her enemy. At first I thought he was sending magic through her plants to attack her but then I realized her green magic was pulling the shadowy magic out of him.

As I watched her overpower the mayor, vines shot up from the ground in front of me and wrapped around my arms and legs. I began freaking out and started to shout at Alice because I thought her spells were getting carried away but then I felt warm energy begin to fill me up. I looked at the others and saw the same thing. She was literally draining the power from our enemy and using it to revitalize us!

Alice waited until there was little left of the former mayor's body. After maybe only a minute of draining, the body became shriveled and parts of it started flaking off. I could actually see the shadow creature inside moving around and starting to leak out. I think if Alice hadn't been using magic to reinforce her plants, the creature inside would have been able to escape.

After a little bit longer Alice suddenly pulled every plant away from the monster until it was just floating in the air. A second later she struck it with an extremely powerful blast of green magic, completely vaporizing it.

As soon as the creature was killed, the remaining fires that had been illuminating the cavern went out. Dorothy then relit some of the small trees with her magic. I guess I hadn't thought much about the fires that had been burning but I wondered if our enemies had been trying to combat Alice with fire earlier.

The vines stayed on us a few moments longer to feed us the last bits of energy it had stolen before retracting back into the earth. I was relieved to see that the burns I had received earlier from the demon were healing up. I had to wonder if it was because dark magic was used to heal them but I didn't press the matter. After finishing the creature off, Alice turned back to check on Glinda who was awake and starting to stand up.

I was left speechless after the display I just witnessed. Everyone else ran to Alice, including the researchers who had been hiding back in the tunnel the whole time. They were really good at staying out of the fighting and I was thankful for that. If they'd become hostages I don't think all of us would be leaving this place alive.

Chapter 16

When we finally made it back to the surface, we were less than excited to see that it was still nighttime. "I feel like we've been down there for ages," Glinda said as she created a handful of smiling pixies to guide through the darkness. Fortunately, we could see the moon and the stars which meant the threat of shadows had been either drastically reduced or defeated from here completely. I really hoped it was the latter.

We were on our way back to Linareus, kind of casually strolling down the road, before we encountered stray shadow creatures. "Ugh," Dorothy and Adam both groaned. "Haven't they had enough of us yet?!" Dorothy shouted before releasing an unnecessary eruption of fire magic that brought down numerous trees and created enough sudden light that I had to close my eyes for a moment. Alice scolded her and then used her magic to put out the fire and cause more trees to begin growing in their place.

It took a little while to get back to the city and we encountered a handful of enemies along the way which put us at our inn close to sunrise. The magical healing we had all received kept us going the whole way–even the researchers got some to help them stay moving–but nothing could beat a hot meal and a good night's rest which is exactly what really kept me moving forward.

Upon arrival, the researchers bid us farewell and, after an exchange of hugs and nice words, they left us to return to their respective homes. The cook working at our inn was already preparing breakfast for the guests but we were much too exhausted to partake. As soon as I walked into my room, sleepiness hit me harder than one of the shadowballs from our last fight. The girls ordered us guys to take baths before bed but Adam was quick to speak for us by urging them not to nag us until we had "at least twelve hours of rest, but probably more." Alice, who was the only one of us nearly completely energized, took control of the situation, forcing us to the bathroom, and even stood watch outside until each of us had come out clean.

Later that day, shortly after noon, we were awoken by one of the researchers. I slept so deeply that I don't even remember passing out or dreaming and I was so groggy that I felt as if I'd just fallen asleep only minutes before being shaken awake.

"Can't we do this later?" I asked, rolling back over into my pillows.

"I'm sorry but the mayor insists. We let you sleep a couple extra hours but it's time to wrap things up. Besides, you don't want to ruin your sleep schedule, do you?" If only he knew how irrelevant a sleep schedule was when you're constantly traveling, running, and fighting at all times of the day.

The girls were up and moving before us. Dorothy was crankier than usual but Alice was as perky and bubbly as ever. After all the concern that Adam expressed over her kidnapping yesterday I was rather surprised to see him get so annoyed by her today. Although, he must've needed more rest than all of us and probably wasn't prepared to deal with any sort of playfulness just yet. Glinda was the one that concerned me the most, however. She was as groggy as Adam this morning and quieter than usual. I wonder if she'd pushed her limits too far last night. Maybe we really did barely make it out of there alive.

The mayor had already been briefed completely before we arrived so we didn't have to tell our story. One of the female researchers had apparently gotten only a few hours of sleep before waking up to meet with the council first thing in the morning and she was still in the hall awaiting our arrival five hours later.

"I apologize for not letting you rest longer," the mayor began. "I promise I will give you all the most luxurious accommodations later this evening." Adam was still too tired for any kind of business. "Listen, ma'am, can you just give us our next assignment and let us get out of here?"

"Pardon me?" The mayor replied in a curious tone. Dorothy chimed in this time. "Where are we delivering the next letter and which mayor are we going to 'liberate' this time?"

"You didn't even let me begin," the mayor said. "I know how your journey has been thus far and I must say it sounds rather annoying. Instead of having you kids deliver any messages, I sent guards off to do that. You can rest here for a while before we decide the next move. No more repetitive A-to-B-to-C assignments." My eyes widened at that news. We were beyond thrilled. Finally, a chance to slow down and figure things out!

"Before you all get too excited, just know that you'll still be employed with me. I don't want you to get rusty so you'll be training my soldiers and performing various missions in the vicinity of this city until we can figure out your next quest." I actually liked the sound of that. It was much more relaxing news than we had received in a very long time. "I'll just let you know right now that the idea is to send you north to the battlefields. While the shadow creatures are possessing villagers and political figures across the nation, they still have armies fielded to the northwestern and western territories. I've been toying with the idea of assigning you to a general or other officers at the front lines so you can aid them but it all depends on their specific missions and what they want to do. I also want to give you some kind of freedom of choice so we'll just have to wait a few days and see what our options are."

All of us left that room in a better mood. This mayor was doing so much for us, more than anyone else had since our journey began. She finished our meeting by informing us that messengers had already been dispatched to our home village to assure our families that we were alive, well, and, as she so eloquently put it, "kicking ass." I certainly felt nothing short of royalty after that meeting. After we left, Adam said he almost ran up and kissed her and Alice said she thought of doing the same thing. We all had a good laugh at that one. The best laugh any of us had had in what felt like a very long time.

I didn't think I'd be able to fall back asleep anytime soon after the great news we received but as soon as my head hit the pillow I was out. I awoke close to sunset to the smell of dinner. Adam was sprawled out on his bed but everyone else was in the dining room downstairs eating. There were two plates of food in front of empty seats waiting for us. I let Adam sleep and planned to take him his food after I was done but not before chatting with the group for about an hour.

We reminisced a lot about home but our hearts were now kind of at ease that letters were sent to our families to assure them of our safety. We also agreed on the plan for the upcoming days. The idea of hanging around this nice city and doing some light work was, as Glinda said, "quite a lovely arrangement." I think we all needed this. We'd been so busy for so long. The closest thing to relaxation we'd really had for an extended period of time was our most recent boat trip but there wasn't even anything to do during that ride besides get in a little bit of training.

Adam eventually joined us and scarfed down his plate of cold food before saying any words. "I appreciate the invite," he said to me. I let out a small chuckle and replied, "you looked like a princess and I figured you needed your beauty sleep after all the work you put in." He didn't even crack a smile like the others did. He just took a drink and then asked Alice how she was feeling. "Absolutely wonderful! Thank you so much for rescuing me, my knight in shining armor!" I think she was trying to perk him up because he didn't seem all the way awake just yet. He'd be pretty short all day, mostly with me, and I wondered if that attitude bothered her.

The rest of the evening was rather dull. It was too late to do much of anything in the town besides drink at the local pubs and the only other option was to head to the inn but I wasn't sleepy enough to go back to bed. I decided to go for a walk and let my thoughts wander. I didn't pick a destination, I just walked wherever the roads took me. I saw kids playing in the roads and stopped to join in a small game of kicking a ball around.

I got to reflecting on our journey up to this point and thought about how we were, only a short while ago, when we ventured off from our village each day to explore. I even tried figuring up the time we've spent on this journey but got myself mixed up and ended up deciding it to be about a month or so. It felt much longer than that. We'd come so far since the start of our quest and seen a world that we couldn't have ever imagined. It's been a long, strange trip and yet, I couldn't help but feel that it was still beginning.

Eventually, I began to think about the sword that had come to me. Was it my destiny to receive it? Was it a blessing? Or a curse? Where did it come from and who was the man that last wielded it? *He must've been a brave warrior to sacrifice his life to save the kingdom.* I had so many questions and I wondered if I could ask the mayor of this city, mostly because she'd been the most helpful and informative so far. My next idea was to talk to any elderly persons I found and question them.

I kept on walking about the city until I noticed that the sun had set. My heart immediately began to race and I readied my right hand to summon my weapon. After a few seconds, I realized I was safe and my body was acting out of reflex. I tried calming myself down by controlling my breathing. I guess all the fighting has had more of an effect on me than I realized. I had to wonder how long that would last. Would my heart still race at this time of day for the rest of my life? Even into old age? It seemed as more days passed I was uncovering more questions but no answers.

I went ahead and made my way back to the inn. I felt pretty good after my walk and even more relaxed now that I gotten to clear out the cobwebs of thoughts that had been tormenting my mind for some time now. I hadn't really had the opportunity to just think and it was kind of nice to be able to now. Up to this point, being alone with my thoughts hadn't done me well, but I think all I really needed to do was talk everything out with someone. Even if that someone had to be me for now. Playing the leadership role unfortunately didn't allow me to just pour my heart out to someone anytime I needed to.

On my way back, I found Dorothy and Alice taking a stroll down a side street and making their way towards the road I was on. "Howdy," I greeted them with a wave. Dorothy whispered something in Alice's ear who then started giggling obnoxiously loud. I asked what was so funny as they approached but both girls just waved me off, still giggling (well, Dorothy just smiled, but it was close enough), and kept walking. I stood there, slightly stunned, for a moment and then shouted, "hey!" And chased after them.

I made it back to the inn rather quickly since I was forced to jog to keep up with the girls who thought it was funny to find ways to tease me the whole way back. Dorothy even went so far as to use a weak curse spell to slow my legs down once. My only thought was that I could definitely give them temporary blindness with the light from my sword if I ever reached them.

Glinda, Adam, and Eric were having tea on the balcony that hung above the patio outside our inn when I arrived. She had dragged them shopping but the idea ended up being a tad unfavorable for her because they passed weapons and armor shops on their way back so the guys forced as much boredom and annoyance on her as she had on them. I saw that the money we had received from our last assignment treated them well because Glinda had on a colorful new outfit and the guys had new weapons and light armor. I was kind of envious because I wanted to shop around for a new sword but there was no sense in that because I already had the best one I was sure to find. I guess it was just the feeling of upgrading that I craved. Of course, I was grateful to have such an awesome blade, but I did enjoy the satisfaction of finding the coolest new equipment after searching around. I supposed I was stuck with this one weapon for the rest of my life and that was a rather bittersweet feeling. I had to wonder if this was what marriage felt like.

Eric asked me if I'd help him break in his new spear when I joined their table. "Don't bother," Adam interjected. "Superhero over here would cut you in two, spear and all."

"His sword is powerful, but not that sharp," Eric replied. "I would enjoy a solid challenge."

"Your best challenge would be these two razor-sharp blades right here," Adam said as he patted his new swords that lay on the table in front of him.

"I've wrestled you more than enough times. I wouldn't want to break another rib."

Adam smacked his hand on the table and pointed at Eric. "You're just lucky we didn't have a referee that time!"

Eric only laughed while Glinda spoke up, "exactly. From now on, I watch every fight. Boys have no sense of self-control." Then she sighed, "my work is never done."

I told Eric we'd have a go at each other in the morning. Him and I have never really fought, and I haven't even lightly sparred with anyone in quite a while so I was actually pretty excited to go a round or two with him. For tonight, however, my only appointment was with my pillows and blanket.

Chapter 17

The next morning started off pretty interesting. Actually, very interesting. I woke up so much more abruptly than ever before because a bag was being forced over my head at the same time ropes were binding my wrists and ankles. A rope was even put across my mouth, outside of the bag, and tied behind my head. I wasn't carried very far before I summoned my sword in my hands. I didn't even think of an attack to use I just forced as much energy to the blade as possible. The light seeped through my bag and, even though it came from behind me, I still felt like I was facing the sun. My attackers must have been severely blinded. I was about to try and make the energy explode out in an area attack until I was struck in the back of the head. Everything was black after that.

I heard the sounds of birds chirping before I opened my eyes. My head was throbbing and it didn't help that I was laying on my back on some firm surface. I didn't want to move but a bug landing on my face was enough to get me to crack my eyes open. Small rays of light poked through a green mist above me. I had to blink a couple times before my eyes adjusted and began panning out the details of my surroundings. I was in a forest. Now the birds and bugs started making sense. But why?

"Hey, pal, you alright?" A voice called to me from nearby. I rolled to my side to face the direction of this new, deep voice. I wasn't sure if my eyes were still trying to adjust or if I was hallucinating but it looked to me like there were a handful of grown men sitting up against the trees near me. "What's going on here?" I asked the group. "Why did you bring me here?" I summoned my sword, ready to force out the answers.

"Whoa now, buddy," the man closest to me raised his hands up to show he was unarmed. "We're all in the same position. We were kidnapped and woke up here." I didn't believe him and stood up, prepared to attack. The rest of the men stood up as well with their own weapons.

I evaluated the threat and decided there was enough of them that I probably wouldn't make it out unscathed and that I wasn't ready to take the life of another human, even if I had to. I retracted my weapon and let everyone calm down before we had a discussion about this strange turn of events. "The only information we have is this," the man told me as he handed over a dirty document that he claimed was attached to his tree when he awoke earlier.

The note said we were to work together and find a way out of the forest within twenty-four hours with every person and all of our equipment. "The mayor mentioned to my friends and I the other day that we'd be helping soldiers with training," I started after finishing the note. "Are you guys soldiers?" The men all nodded. *So that's what this is about.* I hadn't expected to be without my friend for this. I wondered if my friends were going through similar exercises.

My team and I, all eight of us, ran into trouble numerous times during our training. The men I was with were all leaders of some sort and had a variety of tactical and survival knowledge. Unfortunately, none of that mattered because most of our mission ended up being focused on who the leader should be. Every time someone would step up and take charge, he would be undermined by another who thought their ideas were better. It was a constant power struggle that I could not, for the life of me, alleviate.

We spent hours backtracking and moving in circles until twilight when I finally spoke up. I tried explaining how ridiculous they were being and that a kid like me shouldn't have to give them any sort of coaching. In the middle of my speech an idea struck me: "why don't you guys elect a person to be in charge?"

At first, I thought my idea was golden and that they would run with it. Things began with each person giving a reason why they should be in charge of this mission because of whatever skills and experiences they had. All of that started off fine until it turned into one huge argument and even some shoving matches.

I had to draw my sword and create a burst of light to get them to stop. Once I had their attention again, I suggested that we would follow the lead whoever held the highest rank. In my mind, that made the most sense. Unfortunately, two men held the same rank above the others and one person claimed to be from another unit that was completely separate and that the others' ranks didn't hold power over him. Then came more arguing.

This went on past sunset. When I noticed the sky get darker, my heart began to race again. This time, I wasn't within the safety of a populated city and my friends were nowhere to be found… and neither was I, technically. I instinctively forced my blade to glow brighter and scanned my surroundings.

The men stopped fighting when they saw what I had done but I didn't hear any of their words; I was more concerned with what my sword was doing. The light produced from my blade created long shadows behind every tree, rock, cliff, and hill. Additionally, I knew I couldn't shut my light off because none of us would be able to see then. We were trapped by the darkness in an unknown location.

Hours later, deep into the night, we found ourselves no better off than before. I was up front with my sword glowing brightly enough to see everything within about ten meters. That is, everything that isn't being concealed by shadow. My light was indeed bright, but nothing like the sun. My light didn't have the power to illuminate the entire forest. Even if it did, and I honestly had no real way of knowing, it would probably require a considerable amount of energy that I might not be able to control or it would drain me before we found safety. It was too much of a risk to experiment with right now.

I assumed the men appointed me the leader once nightfall began since I had the only light source and because they were too busy to take any time to create torches or a fire. All I did earlier was tell them to follow me and they did. I guess they had no choice since the mission required all of us to stay together to finish.

I had no clue where I was leading us, just that moving was better than sitting and waiting. Besides, if we just walked in one direction, there was a chance that we might find a cave or a way out of these woods or anything different at all. At least if we moved we had a chance at *something*.

I had enough magic in me to keep me trekking all night long but eventually, the men needed to rest. It had been a long day and they wore themselves out from all the arguing. I decided to let them sleep until sunrise while I kept watch. It would be risky because we started this quest in the morning so sleeping until sunrise would be cutting things pretty close but it was a necessary risk.

I used magic to keep myself awake for the hours until sunrise. It was incredibly boring and a few times I thought about waking the men up to move with some lie about hearing creatures closing in on us. The fear might get their blood pumping enough to travel but who knows how long we'd really be out here. After all, there was no information regarding the completion or failure of this mission or quest or whatever it was.

My daydreaming helped the hours pass by at a decent pace. To entertain myself, I imagined up a number of scenarios that would never happen. I distracted myself quite well because the entire sky had lit up by the time I noticed it was daytime. I dimmed the light from my sword which I had stabbed into the tree next to me and woke the men up. They took their time stretching and getting themselves ready to go and, after about ten minutes or so, we proceeded to move out.

The sun was high in the sky when we found a dirt path running through the forest. By judging the movement of the sun we decided to take a right down the trail. Our decision ended up being the right one because not even an hour later we found ourselves at a cobblestone road. Travelers informed us that it would take us to Linareus if we went south and we even found merchants with bread. None of us had eaten in a day and a half so we were definitely ravenous. Luckily, we were able to pool just enough coins together to buy four loaves of slightly stale bread.

A city guard was awaiting our arrival when we reached the city. "You're late," he said to us as we approached. Our group was escorted to the barracks where we were scolded by a furious captain. We failed our mission and thus would each be receiving a more strenuous exercise next. As the men left the room, I was ordered to stay. "Look, kid," the captain began. "I don't really have much authority over you so I can't force you to partake in the same punishments as the soldiers. You and your teammates are just supposed to help guide the men and, from the report you just gave me, it sounds like you made sufficient effort to do just that. You'll probably be tasked for other training events soon but for now you're off the hook."

I asked him what happened to the rest of my friends and he informed me that they all went through similar exercises but with different outcomes. They were released from duty earlier and that I would have to go about finding them on my own.

My first inclination was to get some food. I was assured that my friends were alright so I focused on filling my belly and maybe even getting a nap. Eric and Dorothy were waiting for me when I arrived at the inn. They told me about each of their experiences and how successful they had been. Eric was the quickest one out of our team to return to the city and Dorothy came in third place. Alice was second and Glinda was fourth. Adam was the last to arrive before me but even his group made it on time. Judging from their stories, though, it sounded like I had been stuck with the most unruly men.

The three of us walked around the district until we found a restaurant that sounded pretty decent. All of the places to eat in the city had menus stationed out front for the people to read as they passed by. The place we chose was run by an old couple and served fresh vegetables from their garden behind the building and fresh meat from a farm owned by their grandchildren. I don't know if it was because I was starving or if the food was really that great but I thought I was going to faint from the explosion of delicious flavor in my meal. Thick, juicy steak that was cooked to perfection filled up half of my plate. An assortment of cooked vegetables were piled up on the other half of the plate and the steam coming from them intoxicated my senses. A second, smaller plate was brought that carried a thick pile of mashed potatoes with brown gravy oozing from a dip in the center. Every bite was like tasting food for the first time and I nearly cried as I chewed it up.

The next several days were a mix of busy and boring. Some days would be full of training sessions with the city guards from early in the morning to sundown and other days would include very minimal training accompanied by much downtime. We eventually made another trip as a group to the university and met with our researcher friends who gave us a special tour of the entire facility. Another day, we actually got together at one of the training grounds and practiced our skills with just the six of us. We tested out different variations of our attacks and fighting styles and put our bodies to the test so we weren't at any sort of disadvantage the next time we got stuck with a powerful enemy, like the fire demon who might still be hunting us.

After a week or so of hanging out in Linareus, we were called to the town hall. Our next assignment was ready.

"So here's the deal," the mayor began as we took our seats before her. "A few of the officers up north would be glad to receive your help. Armies of darkness have been gaining ground in the northwest and your skills could prove valuable. I'm not going to assign you any place to go but I can make recommendations if you'd like." I looked at the others who nodded at me and agreed we should hear her out.

"There are two generals and two colonels who have agreed to utilize your powers in their current missions. You are free to help them all or as many of them as you'd like. You can even split into two or three groups. I know a couple of these officers personally. One in particular, General Amber, is a good friend of mine. She is extremely strong-willed and usually gets whatever she wants, on the battlefield and off. You won't find a better mentor or partner, in my opinion."

"Where is she stationed?" I asked.

"About four-hundred kilometers to our northwest in the city of Alvia. There are highways that will take you directly there in close to three days. Currently, her army is fighting to win back the town of Salamanca which is fifty kilometers from the northeastern border of the kingdom of Lilliput, our neighbor."

Lilliput. I haven't heard that name in a long time. Growing up, we got minimal education on geography because it wasn't really necessary for our tiny town. All I knew was that, outside our kingdom of Kepania, there's a much smaller country to the west called Lilliput that heavily utilized the ocean. To our northwest, beyond a thick mountain range, was another country but I couldn't remember the name of it. Like the capital of Lilliput, it was hard to pronounce and thus difficult to remember.

We accepted the mayor's proposal and then discussed with her preparations for leaving at sunrise with some of the city's best horses. "We are beyond grateful for all you have done," the mayor told us before we left. "I wish you heroes and heroines the best of fortune. I hate that you have to endure all of this at such a young age but your power has grown beyond anything we adults are capable of. The soul of this kingdom is in your hands." Her words were powerful but kind of scary. It was kind of frightening that such a responsibility rested on our shoulders. I guess that meant we had to be successful, no matter what.

Chapter 18

A handful of shadow minions piled up against a pair of huge doors. They tried their best to open them but there wasn't enough time. Heavy fireballs from Dorothy exploded upon them before Eric, Adam, and I struck them down. One swing for each creature that wasn't killed by the fire. The doors were made of thick wood but Alice was able to weave her magic through the grains and cause them both to explode open.

We burst into the room, annihilating every moving thing our eyes could catch. A few more of the long, lanky, rubbery monsters were there to greet us but we bowled over them with no more difficulty than the usual pawns we encountered. Their leader was standing at the altar when we finished off its subordinates. It was a large, smoky being that seemed to use the smoke to float above the ground. The wings on its back resembled a bat's and its arms ended in sharp talons.

As we approached our final enemy, the monster summoned a small cyclone of dark energy and sent it toward us. All of us split around it but Alice stayed put and just raised one hand to summon a vortex of wind inside the dark cyclone and dissipate it. Adam sent a spinning blade from the left side while I fired an arc of energy from the right side. The beast used a large amount of magic to deflect both attacks only to have an explosion of fire erupt from below. While high in the air, Eric's spear, propelled by magic, struck it in the chest, pinning it against the back wall. The creature struggled for only a second before dying and dissolving away.

"Thank you so much for your assistance," a priest said as he kissed both of my hands while on his knees. "How can we ever repay your generosity?"
"Don't worry about it," I told him. "We're glad to help. It's what we do for a living."
"But… you must need money for your travels! Or a place to stay!"
I gazed off into the distance and thought for a minute. The sun would be setting in a couple hours and we hadn't had a fresh, hot meal since we left Linareus yesterday morning.
"Sure," I finally said. "But we'll pay for everything."
I heard someone groan from behind me. It sounded

like Adam. He and the rest of the group knew that we had enough money right now to stay for a whole month so one night wouldn't hurt. The people of the town insisted that our stay be free of charge but it was obvious they had suffered enough already so we paid and I even left a considerable offering to the temple.

We were nearly two full days into our trip to Alvia but decided to make a detour at the town of Alcazar and its main attraction: Alcazar Temple. It had recently been overrun by dark creatures who were converting it into a stronghold. The town had been evacuated but not before many people, including women, children, and most of the guards were killed. The town itself had a minimal amount of enemies to deal with but the temple was beyond overrun. We each tried to count the number of monsters we killed inside but I lost track in the forties. Alice claims she was in the sixties before she lost count and Adam says he was in the seventies. I'm not sure how much truth either of those held because they very well could be competing with each other but I know for sure we were around halfway done liberating the place when I hit forty.

"Were they just weak or are we really that strong now?" Alice asked the group while we all relaxed in a heated pool behind the inn. This was our first time experiencing one and I couldn't express how amazing it felt. It was like all my muscles were being gently massaged and relaxed.

"Don't act like you haven't been admiring my strength this whole time," Adam said to her while flexing an arm.

"You make it look easy after my fire wears the enemy down," Dorothy shot back. This led to more bickering that eventually included me and even Glinda.

"You all can write me thank you letters for each individual heal I've blessed you with up to this point," she told us. "Adam, let me know when you want a pixie to recharge your hand every time it cramps us." We got a good laugh out of her remarks. She didn't partake in the play-fighting too often which made her so much funnier whenever she did. I think she just stayed quiet and absorbed everything to formulate only the best responses.

Our little detour put us behind schedule but it felt good to help out and the easy fights made for a decent stretch. We were still about halfway to our destination so we didn't expect to arrive until around noon the day after next. I got a pretty great nights sleep that night. Mostly, I think, because the innkeeper gave us the best of everything, from food to beds. I was also in a pretty great mood about the progress we had made thus far. Even with so many unanswered questions, I didn't feel so lost anymore. We had done and seen so much in the past however many weeks since leaving home, and our village was receiving word of our safety. Additionally, we found more of a purpose for our work. Getting to choose the front lines of the fight was the possibly the best we could hope to ask for to defeat our enemies for good.

I was very excited to meet this general, General Amber, as well. She sounded amazing. Apparently, she had been a middle-ranking officer during the last war with the darkness but when her commander broke down she immediately took over his position and saved the entire unit and numerous civilians. She was promoted to general after the war and she been recognized as one of the most honorable, reliable, and prestigious knights in the kingdom since then. I hoped to learn as much as possible from her experiences and leadership but I also really hoped she could give me more information on the previous owner of my weapon. I think the latter is the main reason I was anticipating our meeting so much.

The next day was pretty uneventful but we did get to see much of the beautiful countryside and stop at some unique towns along the way. The lands we passed through resembled our homeland if it had more hills. Fields rolled on for miles and few trees covered many of the areas we saw. The architectural style of the villages on this side of the kingdom was much different than back home, though. The buildings were made of mostly stone whereas back where we're from they are mostly made of wood. The buildings also looked much older compared to the eastern coast. I found out from one villager that this part of the country was actually one of the oldest regions and that many buildings and villages date back to the beginning of the kingdom.

We played games and made up dozens of silly scenarios to pass the time. We tried to make as few stops as possible after Alcazar to keep close to our arrival time. A messenger had been sent the night before we left Linareus but we were already running late and felt it to be more than rude to keep a general on the battlefield waiting for valuable assets.

When it came to the late afternoon, we ran into another slight inconvenience. About a dozen orbs of dark magic appeared and circled around us. Black smoke was coming from them as well as a purplish glow. They seemed so... familiar. "Hey..." Dorothy started. "Are these..."
"More of the things from outside Ruciam!" Glinda shouted before creating a dozen pixies to attack them all.

As the pixies struck, they all popped in a cloud of smoke, killing their attackers. Then they reappeared, only this time spinning around us. I was too busy watching them and waiting for something to happen so I didn't notice the fireball headed straight for us until the last second. I looked up as it approached my face, intense heat hitting me first. Luckily, Dorothy sensed the magic first and saved me by shooting the fireball with a spell of her own and using magic to knock me off my horse.

Standing, or maybe floating, on a hill in the distance was the fire demon! Dozens of shadow minions surrounded him as well as what looked like possessed animals from the nearby forest. "Girls!" I shouted before kicking my horse into gear. Dorothy sent out fireballs and Glinda released pixies while Alice worked on animating the vegetation and the ground itself.

I had no idea how we were going to beat this thing because nothing ever seemed to work. My powered-up weapon couldn't even finish him off but we all seemed much stronger now so I was confident we could at least beat him down enough to lose him in the woods. I hoped that if we could just make it to Alvia, we would be fine.

There girls' efforts eliminated a vast majority of the small army in front of us. I fired off several waves of energy at the demon to push him back and give us time to kill off the rest of these beasts. The shadow creatures were as easy as usual but the possessed animals were as strong as elite-level monsters. It felt weird to be dueling animals but the dark energy radiating from their eyes and mouths made it easier to mark them as enemies. A super-powered buck managed to kick me in the chest with both back legs and send me off my horse and through the air. I landed at the base of the hill with all the wind knocked out of me and what felt like broken ribs. I wasn't even sure if my heart was still beating. Glinda, however, was already rescuing me with a couple spells.

Adam had ditched his horse and cut down the enemies in his path quickly so he could get straight to the demon who had turned both hands into fiery blades to match the two swords coming for him. I yelled at Adam to warn him about the demon's fire but I was too far away so he didn't hear me. If he did, he just flat out ignored my words. Eric heard me, though, and relayed the message as he closed in on the possessed animals closest to the demon. Adam was managing to hold his own and, from where I was, he didn't seem to be getting burnt but I was sure it was only a matter of time.

By the time I recovered and finished off the buck that had attacked me before, I was ready to join my friends. The demon had extended the length of his bladed arms to match the length of Eric's spear. Adam was using magic to increase the speed and power of his swings but even though the demon was made of fire they couldn't cut through. It was as if something solid was beneath the flames preventing a clean slice.

Alice was nearby, ready to try something new. A small creek was running along the other side of the hill and she was using her staff to help her manipulate the water. As soon as I got an opening, I released a couple light attacks to distract the demon from his two immediate attackers. Eric managed to pierce through the demon's midsection from behind but it seemed to have no effect. The beast backhanded Eric in the chest and sent him flying down the hill. I saw blood, too, and wondered if the edge of the demon's bladed hand made a connection.

Glinda was on the opposite side of the hill so she sent forth a handful of pixies to attend to Eric before running over to him. I took Eric's place by Adam's side while Dorothy moved for a good position to fire a number of magic missiles and shards of ice. We didn't have to keep the demon busy for long because Alice was able to quickly get a handle on the running water. Adam and I ducked out of the way as a rain of heavy orbs of magic-infused water crashed down on the demon.

Unfortunately, the water had little effect on the flames. He was definitely otherworldly because no amount of attacks seemed to harm him. None, except for light magic. "Glinda! He's weak against light magic!" She didn't need anymore information, I think, because she'd seen me push him back before with the magic of my sword. In a matter of seconds, scores upon scores of pixies swirled around the monster, firing little shocks of light all over its body. We heard the deep, creepy voice roar in either pain or anger.

I powered up my sword, expecting him escaped the vortex. Instead, however, he attacked them all at once. An enormous explosion of fire annihilated every pixie around him, and sent Adam, Dorothy, and I falling downhill, and even took off a chunk of the hill's crest. I looked up to see the demon brimming with firey magic. And he was facing Glinda.

I didn't even get the chance to call out to her before he darted through the air with both bladed hands out. All I saw was a bright flash of light as he connected with her body and took her downhill with him. All of us ran after them as they continued onto the highway. They were traveling much faster than we could run but none of us wanted to send any ranged attacks after them for fear of hitting Glinda. Alice made some effort to slow them down, though, because a number of vines popped out from the ground trying to grab ahold of them but to no avail. Even Dorothy conjured up her Despair spell to slow the demon down but she couldn't control it very well while running so it didn't help things any bit.

Before we could even close in on where they finally stopped, we saw another flash of light. And then another. And another. The demon was backing away with his arms up in defense as Glinda kept stepping toward him and releasing blast waves of light energy. Her eyes were glowing with a bright, yellow light as she continued pulsing out blasts of magic. The demon tried to counter with a burst of fire but Glinda deflected it with one hand and shot him with a dart of light that went straight through his body.

We all stopped a ways away to watch this amazing new performance from our previously violence-averse healer. She struck him with a few more light darts and then powered magic in each finger. He didn't even have a chance to stand back upright before she flung ten darts directly at him. He wailed in pain before shooting a cloud of smoke from his body and flying off into the forest.

We all looked back at Glinda whose eyes slowly faded back to normal. She was out of breath and seemed a little surprised with herself. "I'm so sorry," she told us as we approached her. "I don't know where that came from or even that I was capable of something that." Alice gave her a small healing spell to pick her back up as we all congratulated her amazing efforts. I started to wonder why none of us were suffering the same kind of lasting pain I had endured before from this demon's fire. I was going to ask the group if they had any ideas but I missed my opportunity.

"We should go after him," Adam suggested, looking off towards the forest.

"I agree," Eric said. "It's very weak and we know how to defeat it now."

"But…" Glinda began. "I really don't want to do that again. That took a lot out of me and I'm not exactly sure how I did any of it in the first place."

"Just think about it," Alice said, putting an arm around her. "We still need you to protect us from taking anymore damage. And who knows how much more trouble he is capable of in this world? He's gotta be stopped now while we have the chance"

Those words seemed to work because Glinda finally agreed to help finish it off.

The forest was dark and dense. "Keep your eyes peeled," I told the group. "This place looks like a breeding ground for shadow creatures." Glinda sent forth a number of pixies in all directions to keep a look out for traps or an ambush.

I knew we couldn't spend too much time here because we were already well behind schedule but this demon seriously needed to be defeated once and for all. It was important that we finish this here and now. The general would understand, I hoped.

It wasn't long before we were attacked by monsters of darkness. Canine-like beasts attacked us with extreme ferocity. They were fast on their four legs and bit very hard. I thought one was going to bite my arm clean off at the forearm. All of us except for Glinda and Alice suffered at least one wound in the fray. This environment was perfect for Alice who eventually got annoyed with the quick movements of our enemies and wrapped all of them in bramble vines at one time before crushing them completely.

We continued on, running into various other creatures along the way. The only thing that informed us that we were going in the right direction was the obstacles that confronted us every so often. After what seemed like an hour or so, we found ourselves at a clearer part of the forest. There was a very large boulder at the opposite end of the clearing and a small waterfall that fell into a decently-sized pond. A number of stumps dotted the area which made me believe that this wasn't a natural clearing.

We were greeted with a thunderous roar as we stepped inside. The demon appeared on top of the boulder and a large creature resembling a bear joined him at his side. *I would like you to meet Auguseto, the Forest Guardian*, the demon said to us. The bear growled at the mention of his name. With a gesture to us from the demon, the bear began barreling after us. When he got closer I realized that he was by far the largest bear any of us had ever encountered before. He was covered in multiple scars that could only be from years of fighting–probably to defend this place or uphold his title. Now, he was obviously possessed by the demon and had gone from the forest's greatest protector to its worst nightmare.

The first attack was a powerful swipe from a claw directed towards me. I managed to avoid it but an entire chunk of the earth was swept up behind me.

Dark magic came from the tips of the claws with each swing and my back unfortunately caught the ends of that energy. It felt like knives were cutting in deep and the pain caused me to have trouble landing squarely on my feet. The demon appeared before me as I gathered myself together and gave me a strong blow to my new wound that sent me into the air.

Alice's vines caught me before I could land and Glinda's aura spell fixed me up over a short amount of time. Eric caught the bear's attention when he stopped a swipe clean with his spear. He was empowering his muscles with what little magic he had in him and was able to match the bear almost blow-for-blow. The beast became very obviously angry that another creature wasn't backing down before its strength.

Alice assisted me with the demon by first taking control of the water from the pond. We already knew that water had little to no effect on the demon but maybe, hopefully, it weakened him slightly because, at this point, anything was better than nothing. Glinda eventually created two-dozen pixies to watch over Adam and Eric so she could attack the demon. Dorothy stayed with the other guys and pelted the bear with a combination of fireballs and magic missiles.

When the demon saw Glinda, he immediately focused his attacks on her. Alice caused brambles to wrap around him in an effort to slow him down but he just burnt his way through them. Glinda was either waiting until he was closer or was having trouble conjuring the spell again because it wasn't until the demon was only a couple meters from her that a blast wave of light magic burst from her body and pushed him back far enough for me to make a connection with my blade. My powered-up sword cut clean through an arm and a leg causing the demon great pain. He then exploded fire from his body and sent me into a tree.

My face and arms were severely burnt. I howled in pain thinking I was going to die. Alice and a couple pixies tried to fix me up but nothing worked. "Why isn't anything working?" Alice wondered. I barely managed to get out the word "drain" in between screams. That was all she needed. The amount of time between my one word and the vines that healed me could have been a whole year for all I knew. The pain coursing through my body was beyond unbearable. I may have even passed out, I don't know. It was the worst experience I'd ever had, I thought. Luckily, Alice was quick and I was back on my feet in time to see Glinda pushing the demon back against the boulder with her magical darts.

To my left, the possessed bear, temporarily held in place with Alice's vines, was bringing trees down to get to Dorothy, who wasn't letting up her assault. It seemed, however, that her efforts were just angering the beast. Her and the other guys seemed to somewhat have a handle on the creature so I went to join Glinda and Alice with the demon.

The demon pelted Glinda with a barrage of fireballs but Alice took up the role as her main line of defense, using green magic spells to deflect any and all attacks. While the demon was distracted, I powered my blade up with as much energy as I possibly could. So much magic was filling my sword that the light grew to resemble the sun. I had to close my right eye because the brightness was even affecting my vision.

The power of my blade grew so magnificent that my entire sword was almost too heavy to hold. I had to refocus my mind onto controlling all the magic that was flooding into the blade. I started to get a headache but brushed it away and told myself to focus. *Just... FOCUS*!

I thought about my friends, family, and all the innocent people we'd met along our journey. I was determined to defeat this enemy in one blow to protect all of them. No longer would he cause anymore pain. Then I remembered the nice men who were so very willing to help us back in Ruciam. He had murdered them to get to us. I refused to allow this unholy monster to cause anymore pain.

From my anger and the sheer weight of my sword I unintentionally screamed as I charged the demon. Glinda and Alice ran back and covered their eyes. Even the demon seemed to cower as I brought my sword above my head with both hands. My weapon was so heavy but I didn't allow gravity do the job, I used my own personal magic to strengthen my arms and unleash all the energy I had in myself and my weapon. I brought the sword down with everything I had, squarely at the demon's head.

In the brightest flash of light ever seen, I heard the demon scream one last time before its bone-chilling voice faded away. I think I even felt his presence dissipate in the light. I wanted to make sure he was gone so even after my blade came down I continued to dish magic out through the tip of my weapon. When I felt the job was done, I had my blade dim it's glow. Or maybe that happened automatically because I had dumped everything I could all at once. When the light mostly faded away, I was nearly completely out of breath. I dropped to my knees and looked up to see that not only was the demon completely gone, but the boulder he had been up against was split in half and trees behind it were flat on the ground.

I looked to my left to see that everyone, including the forest guardian, was staring at me. Adam finally spoke up, "if you can do things like that, why don't you help us?!" The bear heard that and came out of its trance. It was apparently still possessed because it tried to bite off Adam's head first. Eric and Dorothy resumed their attacks as Adam dodged the chomps.

Only half as many pixies remained over there as before. The bear must've gotten ahold of some of them. Glinda immediately set off a series of spells to heal the damage that had been done to the guys and Dorothy. Alice fired a couple spells before summoning brambles to try and tangle the beast. Eric was tripped up at one point as I made my way over to them. I prepared to fire a magic attack but a splitting pain ran across my forehead that caused me to fall to a knee. All the energy I had just used left me feeling empty. The bear tried to stomp Eric into the group but Dorothy hit him with her Despair curse to slow the attack.

The dark magic radiating from the bear prevented the curse from reaching its full effect but his leg was slowed just enough for Eric to roll away. For the few seconds the beast's leg was slowed, Alice had brambles come from underneath and wrap around it multiple times. The bear was temporarily stuck but it eventually freed itself only after taking a number of hits from Adam and Dorothy.

While Eric, Dorothy, and Alice distracted the bear, Adam and I circled behind. I couldn't power up my blade but I could still swing it around so Adam and I connected all three swords at the bear's upper back. The beast howled in pain, mostly from Adam's attack, which actually drew blood, and turned sharply to backhand us. Adam easily ducked but I was slower to react and just barely caught some of the claw. I went straight to the ground.

"What the hell is your problem?!" Adam shouted at me. I was even slow to get myself back on two feet and didn't respond.

The bear continued to howl louder. We began to sense the magic around it being pulled back inside the beast. The smoky black magic that had been brimming from its body began to vortex all around it. The bear roared as it seemed to power itself up. It's eyes glowed a brighter purple color as black magic erupted from its back. The magic formed itself into dozens of spikes, like porcupine quills. Dorothy warned us that the power she had felt from this monster all along had seemed to double.

"Good," Adam said. "I was getting bored."

I chuckled and replied, "getting your ass kicked is boring?"

"Shut up," he said. "Where's all your fancy power? Get back on the ground; I've got this." I told him I've got plenty of energy left to show him up but he just scoffed and rushed after the possessed forest guardian. There was no way I'd admit to him that I was pretty much completely drained. At least, not unless I landed a devastating, finishing blow to save the day. Then I would gloat to him, as he would to me.

I moved to the right to let him and Eric take all the attention. My blade was still barely glowing and I could feel the light magic coursing throughout so I figured I could cut away at the dark energy on the beast's back and maybe that would help in some way. Anyways, my body was tired so I assumed I would be way too slow up front and just get in everyone's way. I requested pixies from Glinda to assist me in my plan.

Adam did his spinning, tornado-like attack while Eric spun his spear above his head before bringing the blade down on the enemy. Dorothy stopped pelting it with countless little spells and switched to conjuring large fireballs to use the explosions they caused to hinder the bear's movements. Alice took every opportunity she could to use vines to slow the attacks or trip him up while Glinda continued to keep aura spells on each person so their bodies were gradually being healed over time.

The pixies and I went to work on shaving off the quills after Adam and Eric's big hits knocked it off its feet. I had to be careful not only because they were razor sharp at the tips but because I was so weak and I couldn't risk drawing any attention to myself. We managed to cut off a good chunk of them before the bear noticed us and made a swipe that I managed to dodge with Alice's help.

The battle raged on and we began to tire out but the beast was obviously slowing down, too, so we rallied for round two and finally started to get the upper-hand. As the fighting continued, the bear grew angrier and angrier with us. We moved faster than him and landed many more hits than he could. In fact, he hadn't been able to land a direct hit for quite a while. Eventually, his anger fueled his power enough that he was able to spit shadowball spells that brought strong explosions.

Trees began falling all around us as our battle moved in every direction. I had slowed down immensely so Glinda had to tend to me personally with more than just aura spells. Eric eventually lost his spear and was now using his fists and thick branches whenever he could get ahold of any. Alice switched from attacking the beast to keeping Eric fueled so he could nearly match the bear in strength.

While the bear was preoccupied with the insolent human confronting it, Dorothy launched a series of magic missiles that knocked it off one foot. As the bear struggled to regain his footing, Adam lept from one side and carved a huge gash out of the bear's side with both blades. The beast roared in extreme pain and then, as if out of reflex to the surprise attack, caused a number of quills to explode out from his back directly at Adam who was still way too close to react properly.

Some of the quills made a direct hit on Adam's body, sending him falling back a short distance. I wanted to shout and tell everyone to take cover but everything happened so fast that I was unable to get any words out.

Everything happened so fast but the whole world also seemed to move in slow motion. My brain was still trying to register what exactly just happened, so I could only faintly hear the screams from my friends. I was too stunned to react to what I was watching unfold before my very eyes. My brain was trying to tell me that it did not happen. Were the things I was seeing really happening? No way. Not at all. How could it have happened? This had happened before and he was perfectly fine after that. It'll all be okay. He's my best friend, after all, and we're the heroes. The heroes always win, right? You don't just lose your best friend by mere inches or milliseconds. Everything has to be alright in the end, right? Of course it does, because I'd seen him survive many times before. This wouldn't be any different.

Apparently not. Because I was watching my best friend fall to the ground with multiple holes through his body. It all happened so quickly that the blood hadn't even begun to escape him. Not until he hit the ground. The opening in his chest cavity where his heart had just been was releasing the most fluids. And, of course, his eyes were directed towards me. Of course his last image alive is that of his oldest friend in the world just standing in the distance with a blank look on his face. His right arm was reaching out to me when he landed. What could he have been reaching for? To touch me one last time? Begging for comfort? Begging for vengeance? Or begging for help in keeping him on this side of the abyss? I don't think any of those reasons mattered, because his eyes glassed over almost immediately after his body touched the earth.

Glinda had already begun casting healing spells. Her lights were firing in all directions around him like a meteor shower. She was in shock, as well, and wasn't even exactly sure what she was doing except for anything and everything within her power to save him. Unfortunately, her magic was still too weak. Should could mend the wounded but couldn't keep the dead from dying. Eric and Dorothy reacted immediately, pursuing retribution. They went after the murderer with everything they had left, which proved enough to make up for our loss. I, however, was still standing in place. All I could do was stare into my brother's frosty eyes and keep telling myself this isn't real.

None of it can be real. We're the heroes. We're the winners in our own story. We're still back home growing up. We're still hiding our misdeeds from our parents. We're still wrestling with the dogs. We're still racing home at sunset. We're still teaching each other to fight. We aren't here. We aren't fighting for our lives, countless kilometers from home. My best friend isn't dead and I'm not doing absolutely nothing about it.

Chapter 19

Phillip watched in horror as the last ounces of his best friend's soul evaporated into the sky. Glinda continued to dump her entire pool of magic into healing spells. She fell to her knees, bawling. Even her tears sparkled with magic as they fell onto the closing wounds. Alice was beside her, also shedding tears between screams.

"Open your eyes!" Alice screamed. "Your wounds are closed now! Open your eyes!" The last few words barely came out as a squeak. She was crying more and more as the seconds passed and struggling to make her voice work. "I have something very important I need to tell you! But only if you open your eyes," Alice told Adam as she shook his body. When he didn't respond, all of the tears she had inside her came out. She put her forehead on his and cried. Glinda wrapped her arms around Alice and continued crying.

The bewilderment finally left Phillip and all that was left was rage. Eric and Dorothy were beating Adam's killer into and through trees and now Phillip wanted his turn. Ignoring all the pain in his body and the weight of his limbs, Phillip charged the beast with a sword powered up and glowing like a bright rainbow. The magical blade was twice the length as normal and twice as wide, brimming with all the colors of the light spectrum.

The bear was beaten nearly to death when Phillip arrived and split it in half at the middle, along with a couple trees behind it. He took a couple breaths and then swung again. And again. Phillip continued chopping at the beast. Dark smoke shot out onto Phillip's arms and face with each impact, like blood splattering. As his weapon finally powered down, the tears came. Phillip dropped his sword, causing it to flash away, and fell to his knees. "Why?" he asked the minced remains of his best friend's murderer. The tears continued, leaving streaks through the down his face.

Alice was lying down beside a tree, crying into the grass, while Glinda, also crying, rubbed her back. The sun had just set and the light in the sky was gradually fading away as the other three dug a grave in between the two halves of the boulder that had been split earlier. Eric and Phillip used Adam's swords to dig. Their entire bodies ached with exhaustion but they knew their friend deserved the most proper burial that they could make right now. It would be the last time they would see him so they wanted to leave him in the right kind of resting place.

Dorothy, who was always so good about managing her emotions, couldn't fight back all of the tears as she helped make the grave. Occasionally, she'd stop to sob for a moment and then return to her work. Eric had done his share of crying earlier and him and Phillip were now just speechless as ten million thoughts ran back and forth through their heads.

As the darkness descended, everyone continued about their business. Eventually, the team all sat in different places around the clearing to make an attempt at gathering their thoughts. Nobody was ready to leave just yet. When the last bits of sunlight fell on the other side of the horizon, the only light to be found was from the moon and the stars in the sky. Nobody even made any effort at lighting up the area. Nobody even made any effort to move.

Phillip sat against a tree and stared up at the night sky. His thoughts were mainly focused on blaming himself. *I could have prevented that*, he thought. *I obviously had the strength to keep fighting, so I obviously could have been in there helping to defeat that thing before it could kill my best friend.* He continued beating himself up for a long while about being scared and weak. Eventually, he came to the conclusion that this whole situation was his fault. *How many other problems have been the result of my weakness or ignorance?* he wondered. *Was it my fault that dad left us? It couldn't have been mom. No way. It probably was me. It had to be. Why would he want to put up with me? Maybe he saw how pathetic I am early on.* Phillip began contemplating ways to leave the group to avoid screwing anymore lives up. He also began contemplating taking his own life. He thought that maybe that would save more lives if he sacrificed his own. S*o many times along this journey, I have been too weak to fight back. It has always been Adam's job to pick up my slack. What's going to happen now that he's gone? Am I going to get everyone else killed?*

It wasn't long after sundown that the kids heard movement beyond the clearing. Orange lights caught Phillip's eyes, causing him to move his gaze from the stars to the origin of the sounds. "Anyone out here?!" a male voice shouted. A group of soldiers accompanied by a robed figure appeared in the clearing. "This way!" the robed person said. The guard in front then shouted his previous question again. "Over there!" one guard said, pointing at Eric and Dorothy.

"Young masters," the guard began, approaching the two. "Why do you not respond?" After a pause, Dorothy was the first to ask, "what do you want?" "After half-a-day passed from your expected arrival time, we were ordered by Her Grace, General Amber, to search for you. Our wizard sensed a great deal of magical activity in this forest so we assumed, and hoped, it might be your team."

"There are only five when there should be six," the wizard said, looking around. "One has passed."

Nobody said a word. The guards just looked around solemnly at the dismal group. "Come," the head guard said. "We found your horses. We'll get you some food and shelter." The team was reluctant to leave but didn't fight back when the guards helped them to their feet and escorted them out of the forest.

Alvia was a small village. Much too small to be the headquarters of an army. More tents dotted the landscape around the walled town than buildings inside. It had once been a peaceful and thriving farming town that attracted many merchants but now resembled nothing of its past. Most of the buildings were damaged or destroyed when the darkness nearly took the place over before the army arrived. Now, everything was repaired and reinforced with thicker wood and stone blocks.

In the center of the village sat the only two-story building. The bottom half was made entirely of stone and the top half of wood. The roof was shaped like a cone and extended out at its base to protect the wooden walls of the second floor from artillery fire.

Once inside, the team finally got to meet the famous General Amber. When they arrived in one of the meeting rooms, they were forced to wait off to the side for a few minutes while a number of officers huddled around a table and worked on mission plans. Eventually, everyone except the kids and one very large man were dismissed.

"Welcome," the general said with a tired sigh. "I see there really are only five of you now. Please, allow me to offer my sincerest condolences. However, we're at war so mourning the fallen will have to wait until after we win." If the team wasn't already silent from the sad reality of their loss, they would still be speechless in the presence of the general.

General Amber was fairly tall for a female and spoke every word with much authority. She had long, curly brown hair that was tied back. Her face showed many years of fighting, but that didn't hide her natural beauty. However, none of her features compared to the armor that she wore which represented the kingdom's colors in all of its beauty. Made entirely from a deep red mineral that, when eventually asked, she said was a rare stone called Uvite–which was not of this kingdom–and trimmed with gold metal, the armor reflected all light that touched it and even seemed to glow. Her cape was completely white, trimmed in red, and bore the kingdom's emblem of a red, winged bear in the center. The sight of the bear unfortunately sparked only negative emotions in the kids' hearts.

"My officers and I have been working on what we can do with you. We had originally been planning on six, obviously, but five will work just fine. I need you all to get a good night's sleep and wake up tomorrow ready for battle. Loss of life can be hard, I know that more than anyone, but you need to live and fight to honor your friend's memory. Live for you friend. Fight and win for him. Do not let his death be in vain. Stand up for his memory and all that he believed in and use the spirit of your friend to crush all of your enemies. You all are just as capable now, as ever before, of making this world a better place."

Her words should have been inspiring, but there was a limit to what the kids could handle right now and right now they all had something different they wanted to do. Eric wanted to spar with Adam once more. Dorothy wanted to argue with him and lose only to hear him brag and feel good about himself. Glinda wanted to douse him in light and make him feel warm and safe. Alice wanted to hold him and tell him that she loved him. Phillip wanted to take his place in death. Each one of them only currently shared one thought in common: they blamed themselves for allowing their friend to die.

The general sent her new recruits off to rest in their own room at one of the barracks. They were fed with a hot, but simple meal that they could barely eat and then they were each handed a prickly, wool blanket and potato sack stuffed with more wool to use as a pillow. The makeshift cots were hardly more comfortable than sleeping on the ground. None of this was the cause for restlessness tonight, though. There was no time tonight for sleep–this was a night of goodbyes. Goodbye to a best friend, goodbye to a brother, goodbye to a loved-one, goodbye to teamwork, goodbye to happiness, goodbye to ever getting another decent night's sleep, and goodbye to a piece of each of them.

Phillip hoped he wouldn't even wake up if he ever managed to fall asleep. He'd left a piece of himself buried in a random forest far, far away from home. He knew he would have to inform Adam's mother. But how? The general might feel inclined to write to their village but Phillip felt that the letter should be written by the remaining team members. He would have to talk to his new boss about it in the morning. In the meantime, he kept telling himself to fall asleep. He tried to will his brain to shut off. When that didn't work, he tried using magic to knock himself out. He didn't just want to sleep, he *needed* to. If he slept, perhaps he would wake from a terrible dream or perhaps he wouldn't wake up at all. He knew with certainty that this wasn't a dream, so he hoped for the latter outcome.

After what seemed like hours of fighting inside his own mind and listening to sobs from Alice and Glinda, Phillip finally fell asleep.